OPERATOR 5:
THE LEAGUE OF WAR·MONSTERS

SECRET SERVICE #5 ™

OPERATOR 5

AMERICA'S UNDERCOVER ACE

THE LEAGUE OF
WAR-MONSTERS

By Curtis Steele

STEEGER BOOKS • 2020

PUBLISHING HISTORY

"The League of War-Monsters" originally appeared in the February, 1935 (Vol. 3, No. 3) issue of *Operator #5* magazine. Copyright © 2010 by Argosy Communications, Inc. All rights reserved.

CHAPTER 1
BOOMERANG TORPEDOES

WITH SPINDRIFT lashing across its glistening deck, the Patrol Cruiser *Mercury* sliced its way through a running, inky sea. The broken coastline of Maryland lay far behind it now. Ahead loomed vast darkness curtaining the Atlantic—darkness which was complete and empty until sparkling lights appeared in the distance, marking the positions of ships. Across the heaving miles of sea the Coast Guard craft was driving at top speed toward them. The ships were those of the Atlantic Fleet of the United States Navy, arrayed in battle formation.

On the deck of the *Mercury*, clad in dripping oilskins, head bowed against the whipping ocean wind, a young man stood watching the blinking of an electric heliograph which was flashing a message from one of the battleships to another. The message was couched in a double code, yet the keen-eyed young man read it without difficulty. The blueness of his alert eyes grew darker as the words came flickering out of the night:

SWEEPERS REPORT NO FINDING—CONTINUE TO PROCEED WITH CAUTION—ALL OFFICERS MUST REMAIN ON DUTY—TAKE EVERY PRECAUTION AGAINST REPETITION OF DISASTER—RACHARD, COMMANDING.

The Secret League had struck! A pall of terror swept across the capital!

The young man's eyes narrowed with a grim tightness. He knew the details of the catastrophe which had shaken the Atlantic Fleet late that afternoon, though the news had been rigidly suppressed and the newspapers had carried scarcely a hint, for it would have appalled the people of the United States had they known. It was a disaster graver and more fraught with possibilities of serious international complications than any other which had ever struck ships of war in time of peace.

Word of the catastrophe had flashed by wireless from the flagship of the Atlantic Fleet to the Secretary of the Navy in Washington. The Secretary of the Navy had immediately relayed it to the Chief of the United States Intelligence Service. The secret director of all undercover Intelligence operations in the United States had not hesitated in selecting a man to handle the vital case.

His choice was the young man who was designated, in the secret archives of the Intelligence Service, as Operator 5. A copy of that first startling message rested now in a pocket of Operator 5's coat:

> ... SWW... TERRIFIC EXPLOSION STRUCK DESTROYER DECATUR 5:13 EST... POWER STRUCK AT WATER LINE... DECATUR SINKING... MY OPINION DESTROYER RAMMED CONCEALED MINE... MANEUVERS ABANDONED AND MINE-SWEEPERS SEARCHING... ALL POSSIBLE ASSISTANCE BEING RUSHED DECATUR BUT ATTEMPT PROBABLY HOPELESS... RACHARD R.A., COMMANDING....

Following it, a second terse, dismaying communication had flashed through the ether:

… SWW… 5:29 EST… DECATUR FOUNDERED…
HUNDREDS LOST… RACHARD COMMANDING….

The people of the United States still did not know that a mysterious power had annihilated a ship of the Atlantic Fleet, nor that America's undercover ace was riding a gleaming deck to battle a deep-hidden intrigue which was even at that moment threatening the very existence of the nation….

FROM THE bridge of the battleship *Pennsylvania*, Rear Admiral Rachard, Commander of the Atlantic Fleet, watched lights sparkling across the swells as the *Mercury* heaved close. His face was gray-lined; his eyes, bitter. He scarcely moved until an officer entered the bridge-house carrying a message, and his thin lips pressed more tightly at what he heard:

"The mine-sweepers continue to flash negative reports, sir. If there are more mines here they are so well concealed that there is no hope of finding them."

Rachard's voice rasped. "We'll find them! When another ship runs into one—and goes down!"

He peered grimly at the shining battle deck, at movements along the rail. A young man legged over nimbly from the accommodation ladder; following him with eager quickness came a bright-eyed boy. They strode forward together. Rear Admiral Rachard gazed at them in astonishment, descended quickly to meet them.

Operator 5 extended an envelope. The Commander ripped it

open, read a brief message signed by the Secretary of the Navy and identifying the bearer. His eyes shone with surprise.

"I received a code message that you were coming, Operator 5," he said quietly. "I scarcely expected to see so young a man."

Operator 5 smiled slowly. "I am at your service, Admiral Rachard. The Secretary informed you that my identity is not to be disclosed to even your most trusted officers?"

"Yes, of course! But I am still astonished by your youth. Even so, your presence here is vastly reassuring."

Admiral Rachard's keen gaze dropped as Operator 5's hand rose. That hand was marked by a peculiar scar of black and white and gray, formed in the semblance of a spread-winged American eagle. As Operator 5's fingers flexed, toying with his watch-charm, its wings seemed to strain as though for flight. The golden ornament on Operator 5's watch-chain drew the Commander's eyes magnetically. It was a glittering skull and crossbones, its eyes ruby red. In the dim light of the battle deck, it flashed with a significant symbolism.

"And I expected," Admiral Rachard went on quietly, his gaze shifting to the boy standing at Operator 5's side, "that you would come alone."

Operator 5 answered quietly, "This is my unofficial assistant—Tim Donovan."

The boy grinned as Admiral Rachard acknowledged the introduction. He was in his early teens; his face was freckled, his nose pugnaciously tilted. His grin was broad and toothy, his eyes shining with alertness. As he gripped the Commander's hand, Rachard noticed a strange ring he was wearing—a death's-head against a black background, and on the forehead of the skull the mystic numeral 5.*

"You may speak freely before Tim," Operator 5 said. "You may trust him with your complete confidence. He is too young to be a member of the Intelligence Service, though he will become one of us the moment he reaches the proper age. He is as courageous and capable as any operator in the service."

The boy replied: "I didn't do much!"

"You've helped more than you realize, old-timer," Operator 5 answered. He glanced quickly at his wristwatch. "Admiral Rachard, I am in a great hurry. It's imperative that I return to keep a certain appointment in Washington tonight."

THE COMMANDER strode toward his private quarters briskly. Operator 5 and Tim Donovan followed him. He closed the door tightly, turned to regard the pair with intent scrutiny. His voice was a low rumble: "I must warn you, Operator 5, that

---

* AUTHOR'S NOTE: This ring, designed and presented to Tim Donovan by Operator 5, is worn by the boy as a means of identification. All agents of the American Intelligence Service have been informed that by this ring Tim Donovan will be recognized as Operator 5's unofficial assistant. Copies of it are worn by members of the Secret Sentinels of America, but these copies differ slightly from the original in a certain detail which, for obvious reasons, cannot be disclosed here.

we have already done everything possible to discover why the *Decatur* sank. We have no results to report. A valuable unit of our fleet has been annihilated—and before God, sir, we don't know why or how!"

"Your first report stated the belief that a mine had sunk the destroyer," Operator 5 reminded the commander.

"Yes, but—" Rachard shrugged. "If it was a mine, it must have been laid some time ago. It seems incredible that an enemy could have laid mines so close to our coast without being discovered. And our sweepers have been unable to find others. Yet the sinking of the *Decatur* was not an accident. The destruction of that ship means that some nation is making secret war against us!"

"Then we agree," Operator 5 declared, quietly, "that there is danger that other ships will be destroyed—"

Admiral Rachard's eyes blazed. "What? Have you information that—"

"I can say nothing about any information which I may possess," Operator 5 interrupted quietly. "Preparations for war are being made feverishly all over the world, particularly in Europe.* The outbreak of the new World War is imminent. That

---

* AUTHOR'S NOTE: Aside from the storing-up of armaments, various significant indications bear out this statement by Operator 5. Since last fall France has been hoarding war metals and curbing the export of scrap. The French government's fear of the scarcity of material to equip its army recently led President Albert Lebrun to decree a prohibitive export tax on scrap copper, aluminum, zinc, nickel and tin. Aluminum is the only one of these metals produced extensively in France. Officials declared that the action followed

powerful efforts will be made to involve the United States, once the new European conflict breaks out, is certain. The sinking of the *Decatur* may be an attempt to arouse war hysteria even before that war exists!"

Admiral Rachard's gaze became a glare. "We know," he declared, "that European nations are not only arming for war—anticipating its outbreak by training their armies with war games.* It is not difficult to imagine these 'games' becoming actual war even before a declaration has been uttered!"

"We understand each other, Admiral Rachard," Operator 5 declared quietly. "It is no secret that we are menaced by a possibility of war both from the East and from the West. Our naval operations, with which you are thoroughly familiar, openly

similar actions taken by Germany. Germany is likewise struggling to establish her self-sufficiency. In her desperate predicament, she has ordered peat- and coal-operators to undertake the production of gasoline even though fuel produced in this way costs four times the world price. There is also a frantic effort to uncover oil deposits in Germany. Germany intends to become independent of all other countries in supplying gasoline to fuel her engines of war.

* AUTHOR'S NOTE: As long ago as September 11, the United Press cabled the following dispatch to its United States members: "PARIS, Sept. 11.—The French Army, employing, for the first time its latest death-dealing instruments which it will use in the next war, began large-scale maneuvers of war near Bessancon today, fighting off an imaginary attack by a German army from the direction of Switzerland. Marshal Philip Petain was in command. Infantry, artillery, cavalry, tanks and airplanes were employed."

testify to the situation.* But—we dare not jump at conclusions. The situation is too critical. We must act only upon facts."

"The facts in this case," the Commander of the Atlantic Fleet retorted, "are plain enough. Today we were drawn into battle-formation for torpedo practice. Suddenly, without warning, a terrific explosion struck the stern of the *Decatur* and instantly she was sinking. Within a few minutes she was gone. It was not, I repeat positively, an accident—nor was it an explosion *aboard* the ship. It was deliberately planned and the power hit from the sea. We have scarcely dared move since then for fear of striking another mine."

OPERATOR 5'S eyes darkened thoughtfully. "Were the results of your torpedo practice satisfactory?"

"Until the final torpedo was launched, yes. The explosion that rocked the *Decatur* occurred at about the time we expected the last torpedo to hit its target. The *Decatur* was directly behind the *Pennsylvania* at the time. In the confusion, our observations were completely upset. The torpedo missed its mark and so far we have not recovered it."

Operator 5 said, after a moment of thought: "I suggest that we reconstruct the conditions under which the explosion took

* AUTHOR'S NOTE: On August 22 last, the home ports for all units of the United States Naval Scouting Force were ordered changed from the East to the West Coast. The step had been under consideration for some time. The scouting force will be kept on the West Coast, according to an official statement, "until conditions there change." Students of international relationships interpreted this in respect to the strained situation involving Japan.

place. Your ships are still in the same relative positions. I should like you to fire a torpedo at an imaginary target so that I may watch it."

Admiral Rachard looked puzzled. "Very well, if you wish," he said, "though I hardly see how that will be any help."

"There is some reason why your minesweepers have found nothing," Operator 5 answered. "Firing another torpedo may tell us a great deal."

Rear Admiral Rachard stepped to the door. Operator 5's quiet words stopped him.

"Do you, by any chance," Operator 5 questioned, "know of a man in your personnel named Anton Yussov?"

"I have never heard of him."

"Very well," Operator 5 replied softly. "Please issue your orders, Commander."

Rachard opened the door and strode away briskly. Operator 5 stepped upon the deck with Tim Donovan following quietly. A tension tightened the air, a nervous reflection of the startling disaster that had struck the fleet so mysteriously in the open, sun-washed sea. Tim Donovan gazed into Operator 5's eyes with a solemn curiosity, and quietly asked:

"Jimmy—who is Anton Yussov?"

James Christopher—known officially as Operator 5—smiled slowly.

"The man known as Anton Yussov," he answered, "is an international spy—but more than a spy, Tim. We have been interested in him because, months ago, our agents in Europe reported that he had disappeared. I believe that he is now in the United

States, incognito. The information we have on him is startling in the light of what happened to the *Decatur* this afternoon. As for that, Tim—no ring of international spies was ever so dangerous as the Secret League of—"

He broke off abruptly as Commander Rachard strode near. "The torpedo is about to be fired," the Admiral announced. "You will be able to watch from the bridge. A searchlight will follow it. I still can't see how this can help us solve the mystery of the sinking of the *Decatur.*"

"Let us watch that torpedo—and wait," Operator 5 said quietly.

Rachard, his keen eyes studying Jimmy Christopher, led the way to the bridge. There he spoke crisply to an officer who about-faced and saluted. Operator 5 scanned that officer's dark-lined features as orders were given him.

"A torpedo is to be launched immediately, Captain Macklin. Our target is still in position, and we will fire at it. I want you to install a new gyroscope yourself."

JIMMY CHRISTOPHER watched Captain Macklin as he descended from the bridge, and a new darkness came into his eyes. He peered out over the dark water as the Commander came to his side. Below, he saw the protruding torpedo-tubes, the crew in action at them. They pointed at a target—hidden, until the eye of a powerful searchlight blazed, and a white shaft shot out across the swells to flash upon a low-floating object. Then, swiftly, the beam swung back, ready to follow the wake of the projectile as it knifed into the water.

"You doubtless know," Admiral Rachard explained, as the

activity about the torpedo-tubes continued, "that torpedoes become corroded by the sea air in time, and that this corrosion affects their accuracy. Ours, however, are just out of the factory. The gyroscope units, which keep the vertical rudders in a fixed position, are changed after a period of time as a matter of routine. The replacement units are kept in jars, sealed at the plant where they are made, completely immersed in oil. You heard my orders to Captain Macklin. The torpedo we are about to fire should show perfect action."

Operator 5, his eyes narrowed, merely nodded. He watched the crew at the launching tubes intently. He saw the sleek torpedo cradled and rammed into place; he saw the breech locked, and men turn the valves of compressed-air pipelines. Back and forth between the ship and the target, the beam of the searchlight flicked; in a moment the activity ceased. The signal to fire was awaited.

Suddenly, a breathy explosion sounded. Out of the tube the gleaming torpedo leaped, twenty-two feet of shining metal propelled into the surging sea! It dove with propellers whirling, stirring a white wake against the black waves. Carrying five hundred pounds of high explosive, travelling at a speed of more than thirty miles an hour, it plunged through the water while the beam of the searchlight flashed to follow its swift course.

"Keep that light on it!" Admiral Rachard's command rang sharply. "Prepare to see—"

He broke off, peering at the bubbling line of foam shining in the shaft. He gave a quick glance. His eyes widened, and saw Operator 5 leaning forward intently, aware of nothing save the white wake. Again he stared, and blurted in astonishment: "What the devil! Where did they aim that torpedo? It's going to miss the target! It's—steady with that light!"

An appalled silence fell in the bridge-house. The darkness in Operator 5's eyes deepened as he followed the lengthening trail of light. Far out into the surging blackness the line was stretching—and curving! Five hundred yards away, the searchlight playing upon it, the projectile swerved—swerved away from its target and began to trace a circular path.

"For God's sake! No torpedo ever behaved like that before!" Rachard blurted. "It's still turning! It's—!"

Again there was horrified silence. Every officer on the bridge stared transfixed at the amazing spectacle. Every man felt the chill of terror down his spine. Out on the blackness of the sea, the spinning white line continued to bend. Through one hundred and eighty degrees the torpedo plunged on its way— and then again its path straightened.

"God!" Commander Rachard shouted. "God! It's heading back—directly for this ship!"

CHAPTER 2
DUST OF DOOM

"FULL SPEED ahead!" Rear Admiral Rachard gasped the order. An officer sprang to the telegraph and thrust its handle. Far below, in the engine room, a bell tinkled and the desperate signal flashed. Engineers bellowed. Engines roared under suddenly released power. At the stern of the *Pennsylvania*, great screws churned the sea. A tremor passed through the huge ship as she began a frenzied drive through the night.

Operator 5's eyes had not left the white wake of the torpedo for a second. He saw now that it was driving straight for the side of the battleship—a speeding projectile carrying sufficient explosive to send the *Pennsylvania* plunging to the ocean bottom should it strike—a grim robot of destruction had turned upon its masters!

Tim Donovan's small hands instinctively seized Jimmy Christopher's tense arm as he stared. "It's going to hit us, Jimmy!"

Commander Rachard thrust head and shoulders into the tearing, mist-laden wind. His ship was trembling with the full power of her engines, pitching in the heavy swells. He howled downward through flying spray, his voice a strident screech: "Keep that light on it! For God's sake, don't lose it! Captain Macklin! Your rifle, sir! In Heaven's name—hit it if you can!"

Out on the heaving blackness, the course of the torpedo was still marked by the gleaming white line of foam, a line waving back and forth on the surging billows while the projectile continued to drive swiftly toward the battleship. On the deck below, men shouted and quick footfalls sounded. Against the rail, the silhouette of an officer appeared, a service rifle in his hands aimed out over the sea.

Through the water the sleek, flying torpedo flashed, nearing the surface. The officer with the rifle fired—three quick shots that sprayed into the heaving waves. Gasps sounded below: "He missed it!"

Again, below, the rifle snapped its reports. Again bullets

streaked out into the water as the sleek projectile became visible. The officer with the rifle was striving desperately to strike the nose of the torpedo, in that way to explode its charge before it could reach the battleship. The tossing deck and the heaving swells frustrated his purpose. Each slug missed, and the carrier of destruction plunged closer to its mark.

The flagship of the Atlantic Fleet was threatened with doom by its own torpedo!

OPERATOR 5 turned tensely, bounded past Admiral Rachard. He sprinted to the deck, with Tim Donovan scurrying after him. He darted to the rail while spray washed across him, eyes fast on the circle of light that was still following the racing torpedo. He lurched against the rail as the officer with the rifle shrank back, face twisted with the agony of his failure.

"Oh, God—I can't! I can't!" the man screamed.

The torpedo was now plunging directly toward the spot where Operator 5 stood. He glimpsed it nosing out of the water, rearing again as foam streaked behind it. His wet hands seized the rifle from the officer. He swung, bracing against the rail, snapping the weapon to his shoulder. The ship was pitching and tossing; the sea was black chaos marked by the lengthening path of doom. With every muscle tight, Operator 5 leveled the rifle.

Flame flashed from the bore swiftly as the nose of the torpedo reared out of the water again. The report was a coughing sound snatched away by the singing wind, a noise echoed by a terrific explosion that jarred the sea to its depths.

Brighter than the glare of the searchlight, flame leaped out of the surging sea. Flying high, flinging up a lash of water, sending a drenching rain across the deck of the *Pennsylvania*, the fire and power of the exploding torpedo ripped through water and sky. The great battleship jarred with the concussion. Men whirled, cowering from the rail. Officers recoiled from the blinding light. Across the water surged a white-maned wave that slapped violently broadside against the ship and sent men tumbling.

At the rail, Jimmy Christopher clung, hands whitened, rifle lost. Chill water drenched him. He peered up to see the water boiling and the searchlight playing upon a chaos of waves. He whirled about to see Tim Donovan clinging beside him, dripping, white-faced.

"Tim! Are you all right?"

"Jimmy, gee—you hit it!" There was frank admiration in the boy's eyes. "Sure, I'm all right."

A broken sigh passed Operator 5's lips. Men were scampering about the draining deck, drenched to the skin, their faces gleaming wet and white in the deck lights. From the bridge, officers came hurrying. Operator 5 left the rail, his face grim, his blue eyes shining darkly.

Admiral Rachard stopped short, chilled. "By God, sir! You're the best sharpshooter I've ever seen!"

Another officer stepped close, breathing rapidly. "I'm sure glad you took that rifle from me! I was going to pieces. I couldn't have hit it. God, what a close call!"

Operator 5 faced the Commander narrow-eyed. "You ordered Captain Macklin to use the rifle, sir. This man is not Captain Macklin. Where is he? I want to see him at once!"

Rachard peered about grimly. "Macklin!" he snapped. "Find

Macklin!" As men hurried off, he stepped closer. "What the devil happened? No torpedo ever behaved like that one before! You suspected that it might, didn't you?"

"I scarcely expected it to turn directly back on this ship, Commander," Jimmy Christopher replied tensely, "though I did believe that it would leave its course and pass either in front of or behind us. I think, sir, that the mystery of the sinking of the *Decatur* is solved. She was sunk, not by a mine, but by one of your own torpedoes that turned back on her!"

ADMIRAL RACHARD'S face went white. "There is nothing else to think. Thank God you discovered that before we resumed torpedo practice! You have made more headway in half an hour than we have in all the time since—"

"I beg your pardon, Commander," Operator 5 interrupted, "I want to see the replacement gyroscope units that you have aboard."

Admiral Rachard strode away swiftly, leading Jimmy Christopher and Tim Donovan below deck. When they paused, it was in front of metal cabinets, all firmly locked. As he brought out his keys, the Commander paused, his sharp eyes searching Operator 5's face.

"Why the devil did you suspect the torpedo?" he asked. "How is it possible that you—?"

"It is clear enough, Commander," Jimmy Christopher interrupted, "that I have acted upon certain important secret information. I have gathered this information through independent work, and not even my chief knows about it. I can say nothing more now."

"I understand!" Rachard's key clicked in the cabinet lock. "It is perfectly plain why you want to see these—" He broke off short, as the compartment doors opened wide before him, and stared in white-faced surprise.

Operator 5's gaze turned upon empty shelves. He stepped back, and his fingers strayed unconsciously to the little death-charm he wore on his watch-chain. Very quietly, he asked: "The replacement gyroscopes were kept in that compartment, Commander?"

"Yes! There should be at least half a dozen of them in there now. Captain Macklin is in charge—"

Jimmy Christopher interrupted, his voice becoming edged, "Where are Captain Macklin's quarters?"

Admiral Rachard's compressed lips withheld the answer as he turned away. He strode swiftly, with grim purpose, while Operator 5 followed. Tim Donovan paused at the side of Jimmy Christopher when they faced a closed door. Rachard's knuckles rapped on it. When there was no answer, the Commander twisted the knob, and found the way locked. Again he knocked, angrily, and called:

"Macklin! Are you there? Open this door, Captain Macklin!"

Through the slapping noises of the sea beating against the *Pennsylvania,* quiet footfalls sounded beyond the door. They were slow, heavy, deliberate. There sounded the scratch of a bolt being withdrawn, then quicker footfalls turning away. Admiral Rachard's hand went to the knob; but Operator 5 gripped his wrist, stayed it.

Jimmy Christopher opened the door as Rachard stepped

back. He stepped into the officer's quarters, peering at the man across the room. Captain Macklin stood backed to a table, white-faced, lips thin, white showing around the glittering pupils of his eyes. Operator 5 caught the glitter of jars on the table behind Macklin, though his gaze did not shift. Softly, he said:

"Perhaps now you feel, Captain, that the Secret League has not paid you nearly enough."

A sob of rage and grief broke through Captain Macklin's colorless lips. He stepped forward swiftly, and his arm swung up. His whole body trembled as his hand poised to hurl a black, shining object toward Operator 5. His tight muscles strained as he blurted: "Get back! Get back, for God's sake! I'll never stand court-martial! You'll never—"

Black lightning! The glistening object streaked from Captain Macklin's hand as a paroxysm of desperation seized him. Operator 5 leaped backward through the door as the glittering sphere whizzed across the room. He whirled aside as a sharp crash sounded—as fire flared into being with an angry roar!

THE SPLASH of flame burst across the doorway. Blazing liquid spattered with a hollow concussion. Past the sill, fiery drops flew; beyond it a surging, roaring force filled the room. In an instant, choking fumes poured outward, an ear-piercing hiss filled the air. Operator 5's sharp command sent Admiral Rachard and Tim Donovan springing aside while he crouched, peering into the hot heart of the sudden inferno.

"Extinguishers!" he ordered. "Quick!"

A sharp moan of agony came from the flame-filled room before Rachard bawled an echoing "Extinguishers!" The incendiary fluid had spattered upon the walls, across the floor and upon the man who had hurled the bomb. Within that beating hell, he was standing braced against the table, head thrown high, rigid with the horrible agony of the flames enveloping him. From his uniform, fire blazed up around his face—and with a moan he melted down in the blasting heat.

Operator 5 turned as men came running with extinguishers in their hands. He snatched the nearest instrument; he upturned it and sent its sizzling stream into the room. It splashed a clear path across the floor, a path that immediately began to close as new flames leaped up. Beside him, two other officers stood, turning their hoses through the doorway—but it was as though the extinguisher fluid was consumed in the blaze a moment after it emerged from the nozzle.

"Keep back!" Operator 5 warned. "It will have to burn itself away! Keep the fire closed in! Shut the door as soon as I come out!"

He poised to leap across the sill of flame; Tim Donovan cried out frantically: "Jimmy—don't!" The boy groped forward to seize Operator 5's arm—reached quickly, but too late.

Playing the stream before him, Jimmy Christopher ducked into the room. The sizzling foam cleared the way for him only a moment. Flame snarled all around him as he stepped deeper into the inferno which formed a charred oasis around him as he moved. Those watching in horror through the doorway saw him vanish behind a burst of fire.

Tim Donovan peered anxiously through the doorway—until the slashing stream of Operator 5's extinguisher cut through the flames again. It whipped blackness in front of him as he ducked low, dodging toward the door. Under one arm he was carrying a jar which glittered a blackish amber. He leaped across the sill and whirled away, gasping, dropping the tank.

Tim Donovan clutched at his arm. "Jimmy—you're burned!"

"Not badly, Tim!" Operator 5 exclaimed. "The fire scarcely touched me." He straightened, his wet clothing steaming, and his lips curved in a tight smile. "Shut that door! Stay out until that stuff is through burning!" To Admiral Rachard he said in a lower tone, as the door slammed shut: "Captain Macklin had made a provision against his being discovered—and he used it! There will be little left of him, sir, when that fire burns out— and he'd intended that there should be nothing at all left of this evidence."

Rachard's eyes blazed. "By God, sir, I would never have believed it of Macklin!" He turned, howling orders to his men to keep the fire from spreading, and swung back to peer at the jar Operator 5 had brought from the blazing room. "One of the

The Mysterious Stone House In Balkaria.

JIMMY
CHRISTOPHER

replacement gyroscopes! Then it was Macklin who took them from the cabinet! Macklin's work that—"

"We had better inspect this, Commander," Jimmy Christopher said quietly, "in the privacy of your quarters."

Men with extinguishers were playing hissing streams on the

blistering door of Captain Macklin's room when Commander Rachard turned away grimly. Tim Donovan kept at Operator 5's side as they approached the Rear Admiral's quarters. Once behind the closed door, Jimmy Christopher inspected the jar closely.

"Observe that the seal is not broken," he said quietly. "It has not been tampered with. But it is not a genuine United States seal, Commander. It is a clever forgery—as Captain Macklin knew. When we investigate his case, we will find that he jettisoned the original, genuine gyroscopes, and substituted others, like this one."

"You mean that he was the paid agent of—?"

"The tool, let us say," Jimmy Christopher interrupted, "of as vicious a combine of international spies as has ever operated. The man I mentioned—Anton Yussov—a Balkarian physicist, is only one of them. Yussov is not acting for his own government. The cabal of which he is a member is a foe to all governments. This instrument, I assure you, is a product of that man's evil genius."

Operator 5 broke the seal of the jar. From its bath of oil, he lifted the delicate mechanism it contained. Admiral Rachard peered at it closely as Jimmy Christopher gently rubbed some of the oil between his sensitive fingertips.

"In all respects it seems to be one of the genuine government gyroscopes!" Operator 5 explained. "But it has been expertly counterfeited!" He extended his fingers. "Emery dust has been mixed with this oil. The effect of the abrasive is to wear the bearings rapidly as the gyroscope revolves. That in itself would account for the erratic action of a torpedo guided by one of these counterfeit instruments. But in addition to that, the wheel is badly off balance."

HE SPUN the wheel, and the vibration was noticeable. He returned the gyroscope to its blackened oil, and looked at Commander Rachard.

"The combined effects were more than enough to send the torpedo back on the ship that fired it. The operations of a combine of terrorists, the treachery of a weak-willed officer, an instrument which makes a boomerang of one of our weapons of defense—they are all part of the secret of the sinking of the *Decatur*, Admiral Rachard. Order all replacement gyroscopes to be inspected and all counterfeits destroyed. Then you may proceed with your maneuvers without fear that the disaster will be repeated."

Admiral Rachard's great hands formed into fists. "Operator 5, you have saved us from seriously crippling our fleet!"

Operator 5's lips curved in a tight smile. "The danger to our fleet, Commander," he declared, "is little compared to the danger now threatening our nation. We have seen only a small part of a gigantic, diabolical plan that is in operation at this very moment. The real nature of that plan is still a secret. We know only that destructive forces are operating against us—that the purpose behind these forces is to destroy us. Henceforth, every hour of the day and night, we must keep on the alert against them."

He glanced quickly at his watch, turned toward the door. Tim Donovan followed him. He said quietly:

"I have scarcely time to get back to Washington in time

to keep my appointment, Commander Rachard. I ask you to remember that even the closest, strictest vigilance may not be enough to save us!"

The Commander of the Atlantic Fleet had grown pale. Eyes shining with deep concern, his bronze face deeply graven with black lines, he asked slowly: "Is it possible that any ring of spies can become such a serious menace to a nation as great as these United States? Is it possible that any secret power is strong enough to destroy us?"

Operator 5 paused, his darkened eyes on those of the Commander. "Yes, it is possible! The weapon that may be turned against us is war—war that will sweep around the earth to embroil every existing nation—a World War in the full sense of the term, that will inevitably engulf the United States and wipe us, with all other countries, out of existence!"

ACROSS THE swelling, wind-whipped sea the Patrol Cruiser *Mercury* cut its way while Operator 5, oilskins drawn tightly about his slender body, stood on deck and peered through the night. Tim Donovan, at his side, glanced anxiously at him. They had not spoken since leaving the *Pennsylvania*, and now the lights of the Atlantic Fleet ships were twinkling away into the misty distance of the sea. An ominous foreboding kept Jimmy Christopher silent while spindrift flew, while the shore beacons appeared and the *Mercury* slashed on. Clearly he recalled a message that had been delivered to him earlier in the day, a message significant in its cryptic terseness:

Ministers without Portfolio of certain European governments have united in a request that you confer with them on a matter of the greatest importance. You will meet with them tonight, at midnight, at Address K.

Z-7.

At full speed the *Mercury* plunged through the night, carrying Operator 5 to a secret conference—a conclave upon which hinged the destinies of nations, yet which was never to be recorded in formal world history.

CHAPTER 3
THE AWAITED HOUR

N O NOISES of the city reached inside the four walls of the amber-lighted room. Not even the ticking of a clock disturbed its silence. It was long and narrow, hung with tapestries and oil paintings; its doors were massive and strong. Heavy curtains draped its windows. It lay high above the street, on the topmost floor of one of the most fashionable hotels of Washington, D.C.

Its approaches were many. In the ordinary manner it could be reached from a quiet hallway; in addition, it could be entered through rooms at both sides, and through two others from below. A special elevator stopped—when one carried the necessary credentials—at its level. When, on rare occasions, it came into use, it was kept under constant surveillance from outside.

It was a room maintained for extraordinary, unofficial purposes by the United States government; in the secret lexicon of the Intelligence Service, it was known as Address K.

The quiet of this room was disturbed, as midnight approached, by the slow opening of a door. The man who entered was clad in gray; his eyes were a smouldering black sprayed with deep lights like the heart of ebon diamonds; his face was hard and dark-lined. He stood at one end of the room and waited for the hour of twelve to strike.

He was known, even to his most trusted lieutenants, only as Z-7; he was the Commander-in-chief of the United States Intelligence Service.

Again a door opened. Two men entered, followed by two more. From another door four more came in. Through still another, two others appeared. They glanced at their watches, and no word was spoken. Z-7, with a gesture, bade them take chairs. Seated, they waited while the hands of their watches crept to the moment of twelve.

Each man evinced a different racial strain, a different temperament. The attitude each bore, as he waited, differed—eager, hopeful, grim, nervous, patient, bewildered. And all were silent as the seconds ticked past.

The click of another opening door brought them to their feet. Z-7 turned as a step sounded. Into the room strode a young man whose face was masked by a strip of velvet across his eyes—eyes which were an alert, intent blue. His hands were black-gloved. He strode briskly to Z-7's side and paused.

The Chief of the United States Intelligence Service faced the group. "Gentlemen," he began, "let us waste no time. We have assembled here for a common purpose. The man you wish to see stands beside me. I present Operator 5."

The ten approached. Z-7 continued quietly:

"Operator 5, I have the honor to present to you these representatives of ten world powers. They carry no official credentials, but they are not secret agents—each of them has duly presented himself to the Secretary of State. Their presence here is otherwise unknown. They have come from their respective countries to confer with you on a matter involving their governments most gravely."

Indicating each man in turn, Z-7 presented them to Operator 5.

"Sir Lindsay Barker, representative of the King of England. Monsieur Pierre Mondel, emissary of the President of the Republic of France. Leon Maximoff, sent by the Commissars of the Soviet. Signor Veneto Tarento, representative of the King and the Premier of Italy. Mr. Josef Bundes, agent of the President and the Premier of Austria. Mr. August Lodczski, unofficial ambassador of the President of Poland. Count Andreas Karothy, representing the Regent of Hungary. Herr Franz von Benecken und Anhalt, emissary of the President-Chancellor of Germany. Mr. Sakhali Otaru, minister without portfolio from his Majesty, the Emperor of Japan. Sivet Istabar, representing the Grand National Assembly of Turkey. Gentlemen—Operator 5."

NO WORD was spoken as Jimmy Christopher grasped the hand of each man in turn. They stepped back, still facing him. Z-7 continued quietly: "You may proceed, gentlemen, with the assurance that no word spoken here will ever reach the outside world."

The man who stepped forward was Sir Lindsay Barker. His

frank eyes studied Operator 5's masked face as he spoke in a gentle, firm tone: "Operator 5, all of us are aware of the great services you have rendered your country. We have come to enlist your assistance, for we believe that without your cooperation our mission must surely fail."

Operator 5 acknowledged the compliment with a bow.

"Once you learn of our mission, you will pledge your help, I am sure," Sir Lindsay Barker continued. "The matter involves the welfare of your nation, as well as the nation of each of us. We are men whose governments are both friendly and hostile to each other, but to this we give no thought now. We are united in the single purpose of the welfare of all our nations because—"

Operator 5 broke in quietly, "You are united by a bond of fear because all your nations face the threat of extinction!"

Sir Lindsay Barker looked startled. "True," he admitted. "We are aware that a new World War is imminent. At any moment, the first fires of the new conflict may burst out. We are certain that there exists in the world a secret combine devoted to wiping away all national boundaries, of destroying all nations as they exist today, of erecting a single, worldwide dominion.

"This combine plots to use for this purpose another World War. We are still staggering under the load of the last. All nations are in grave economic and political distress. We have been arming ourselves for defense, supposedly, but in reality for national suicide. A prolonged World War will bankrupt every existing government.* This fact the secret combine knows. It is deliberately waiting for the new war to disable us so that it can strike when we lie helpless. This combine, Operator 5, is known as—*The Secret League of Nations!*"

THE MEN facing Jimmy Christopher stared in astonishment. A moment of tense bewilderment passed. It was broken by a breathy exclamation from the British representative.

"Then you know!"

Operator 5 answered: "I have gathered information independently which verifies every word you have said. I not only

---

* AUTHOR'S NOTE: Early in 1934, practically all hope of armament-limitation disappeared from the world. All nations began an armament race at an appalling cost. *The League of Nations Armament Year Book,* issued late last August, declared that in 1933 a total world expenditure on armaments of between $3,471,000,000 and $4,399,000,000 had been made, and warned that, due to depreciated currencies, even this did not indicate the full cost of the world's preparations for war. More specifically, the following developments occurred early in 1934: The United States prepared to spend between $750,000,000 and one billion dollars on building the U.S. Navy up to full treaty strength. Great Britain voted the largest navy budget since 1928—$278,274,000. The government of France authorized a three-billion-franc ($197,400,000) bond issue to pay for additional armaments.

Japan's House of Representatives voted a budget of 2,112,000,000 yen ($633,600,000), of which 44 per cent went to the Army and Navy, an all-time peace-time high. These actions, typical of all nations threatened with war and striving to out-arm each other, give factual basis to the statement made here by Sir Lindsay Barker.

know that the Secret League of Nations exists, but I know that its members, at this very moment, are working within the boundaries of the United States!"

Z-7 was staring at Operator 5's masked face. "Great Scott, you have hinted none of this to me! I know that you have been working night and day, but—"

"I have just correlated my findings, Chief," Jimmy Christopher answered. "Only a few hours ago I was able to piece my information together and learn the full import of the secret plan." He faced the startled representatives again. "I began my work months ago, gentlemen, sifting the evidence that a world-wide plot was in operation.* I did not dream, at the time, what vast ramifications would be revealed.

---

* AUTHOR'S NOTE: A few garbled hints of the cases on which Operator 5 was working reached the press early last October. In Rotterdam, the river police on October 4 discovered a widespread plot of smuggling aliens, mostly Germans, to the United States. On the same day the police in Austria thwarted what they believed to be a plot for a new radical revolution in that country; they seized, from a cyclist courier in the Forisdorf section of Vienna, coded papers instructing the placing of machine-guns at strategic points about the capital for the planned uprising. The plot was attributed to Socialists. On the same day José Grau of the Department of Interior of Cuba, charged that Soviet Russia was maintaining in Paris a propaganda office from which Cuba and other Latin-American countries were being flooded with Red literature, and the International News Service carried to its press members an item reading, "Communism, entrenched in Cuba where it is struggling against governmental authorities in a grim battle for

"I have learned," he continued, "that certain dangerous spies have worked their way into the United States. These men are all exiles from their own countries—men stripped of their nationalities. It is no coincidence that each of them hates nationalism bitterly. There is only one possible answer: They are combined for the purpose of overthrowing existing governments, and that conclusion is verified by a code telegram intercepted by our Intelligence Headquarters here in Washington."

Operator 5 drew a folded paper from his pocket. "This code could not be deciphered by any of our cryptogram experts. Feeling that it was a challenge, I tackled it and succeeded in translating it. It is addressed to an alien whose activities I am investigating—the exile from Balkaria, Anton Yussov. It reads as follows:

"Our work resumes in America! For the first time, our Secret League of Nations will meet within the United States exactly four weeks from tonight. We stand united in the purpose of flinging the United States into the furnace of the war that is coming at any hour!

"The name signed to this amazing message, gentlemen, is that of Luther Sigmond, an international spy, an expatriate from Germany, a terrorist—and one of the most dangerous revolutionists living!"

power, is spreading through vast areas of the Western World." These scattered operations were, according to Operator 5's statement here, part of the same world plot.

M. Pierre Mondel, unofficial representative of the government of France, exclaimed with a marked accent: "Then you are fully aware of the danger we are facing! We can tell you nothing that you do not already know!"

THROUGH HIS mask, the eyes of Operator 5 shone darker. "Gentlemen, I have spent days and nights on end sifting secret reports that have come to our Intelligence Headquarters. You, in turn, have begun your investigations independently, and have arrived at the same conclusions. The Secret League of Nations, composed of the most dangerous terrorists and annihilists in the world, is fostering war that threatens to destroy all our nations. We are facing the most serious threat to civilization in the history of the world!"

There was silence. The ten men gazed intently into Operator 5's masked face. His voice was almost a whisper when he continued:

"The Secret League, gentlemen, is incomparably more dangerous than any ring of spies which ever before operated—a greater threat than any single spy who ever lived. In comparison, the danger of such undercover destructionists as Radi Havara and 'the Red Venus' is nothing."*

Sir Lindsay Barker exclaimed: "True! Our paramount wish is to preserve our nations from the ravages of war and the threat of destruction. That of the Secret League is to encourage the

---

* AUTHOR'S NOTE: Radi Havara, one of the most ruthless international spies who ever lived, is already known to readers of "The Red Invasion." Concerning Operators 5's second reference, the following news dispatch, sent by

conflict and to wipe all nations from the map of the world. We can hold no hope of salvation unless we unite to fight the Secret League."

They waited for Operator 5 to speak. His eyes shifted alertly from face to face. His words came slowly, deliberately:

"Gentlemen, we each realize fully the dread results that will follow if the Secret League succeeds in its purpose. I am as devoted to my country as each of you is to yours, but I warn you that the threat against our nations is nothing compared with

wireless to *The New York Times* from Constanta, Rumania, on September 6 last, is pertinent:

"The attention of Rumanian customs officials was drawn on the arrival of the Rumanian steamer *Principessa Maria* from Istanbul today to four passengers, one of whom was a beautiful woman. They brought twelve luxurious leather trunks with them.

"While customs officials were investigating the contents of these trunks, the woman was seen to be attempting to swallow pieces of paper. She fought desperately when officers attempted to interfere, using boxing tactics and jiu-jitsu. She was overpowered only after long resistance.

"The pieces of paper proved to be a letter from Russian officials, recommending the bearer to Bolsheviks in Constanta as 'one of the best workers for the cause of the Soviets.' Customs officials found the trunks contained … many articles usually carried by professional spies.

"The police had been warned of the activities of 'an extremely beautiful woman spy, generally referred to as The Red Venus.' She is a Russian Jewess, but her name and those of her companions were kept secret by the Rumanian authorities."

the threat against our peoples. Worse than the destruction of our nations, we are facing the destruction of our civilization, our families, our homes, ourselves.

"If the Secret League succeeds in wiping away all national lines, no barriers will remain to bar annihilating hordes from swarming across the face of the earth. This country, for instance, will no longer be protected by its immigration quota system. The lowest of all humanity will come here in a flood. Hundreds of years of progress will be wiped away. The people of this country will be forced down to the level of existence of coolies and peons and slaves!

"That horrible fate, gentlemen, is what the people of the United States are facing at this very hour—a danger you likewise face, though to a lesser degree." *

OPERATOR 5 paused, his eyes shining like blue metal. This is more than a plot by radical fanatics who desire to establish a world community—one single nation. I assure you that behind

---

* Author's Note: That the world's yellow races are breeding five or six times faster than the white races is a discovery resulting from researches conducted recently by Professor Charles Richet, president of the French Academy of Sciences. Of the white people, Professor Richet found, Europeans increase most slowly and the most civilized European countries, the most slowly of all. Shanghai leads the world's great cities in rate of increase, with Tokyo and Osaka following. Within the next ten years the population of the world, not considering the effects of disasters, will increase by 195,000,000. To these, Europe will contribute 20,000,000, the Americas 35,000,000 and Asia 140,000,000.

the Secret League of Nations is a greater and more terrible power. It is, I believe, using the Secret League only as a means to an end.

"If the world community is created—if only one nation remains in existence on earth, who will rule it?"

A stricken silence followed. Operator 5's intent gaze passed from one paled face to the next. The ten unofficial emissaries peered at him in cold horror.

"Great God!" Sir Lindsay Barker's exclamation was a horrified burst of breath. "Do you mean to imply that the Secret League is only a tool of a man who aspires to become the ruler of the world?"

"Exactly!" Operator 5's tone rang. "The Secret League is controlled, not by men like Yussov and Sigmond, but by one far stronger. He is a man obsessed by an ambition to overshadow the conquests of Genghis Khan and Caesar and Napoleon. He desires power greater than that of the President of the United States, the King of England, the President-Chancellor of Germany and the Premier of Italy together—a power greater than the combined strength of all the rulers of the world!"

"But—!" Sir Lindsay Barker stared at Operator 5 white-faced. "What means can this madman employ to gain complete rule of the earth?"

Operator 5 answered slowly. "There is no doubt, gentlemen, that he has provided for a means. As to its nature—I am completely in the dark. But I promise you I will devote every effort to uncover the machinery of the Secret League—and to learning the identity of the man who aspires to world dominion.

Operator 5's words came briskly now. "I ask your complete cooperation. You must return immediately to your respective countries. You must work with all possible speed, with all your strength, to discover and destroy the power behind the Secret League. Once war is declared in Europe, our task will become a thousandfold more difficult. Lose no time! Go to your governments and marshal every resource—"

OPERATOR 5 broke off. Into the quiet of the room came a muffled, clicking sound. Z-7, standing at Jimmy Christopher's side, turned to peer at the side wall. In a carved rosette beside a panel, part of the decorations of the room, a tiny red bulb was gleaming. The Washington Chief addressed the ten unofficial ministers.

"Gentlemen, a message is being sent here by teletype. The instrument is never used except for the most pressing emergency. I ask your indulgence."

Operator 5 remained silent as Z-7 strode across the room. Facing the panel, the Washington Chief pressed a lower leaf of the rosette. Immediately, the red gleam disappeared; the polished

TIM
DONOVAN

section of wood slid away quietly. A cavity was disclosed behind it as the metallic clicking became louder. In the recess sat a tele-type instrument, a strip of yellow paper curling from it as words formed. Z-7 bent forward intently.

Operator 5 saw him stiffen—heard him gasp, "God!"

He took quick steps toward the Washington Chief as Z-7 turned. The eyes of the gray-clad men were smouldering coals. *"It has come!"*

He passed the strip to Jimmy Christopher. The black words

formed a terse, historic message that chilled Operator 5's heart and held him rigid.

...KING GREGOR OF BALKARIA ASSASSINATED... AUSTRIAN PLOTTERS CAPTURED... BALKARIA IMMEDIATELY DECLARES WAR ON AUSTRIA... MUSSOLINI ORDERS MOBILIZATION... GERMANY THREATENS DECLARATION OF WAR ON ITALY... GREAT BRITAIN WARNS BELLIGERENTS SHE CANNOT REMAIN NEUTRAL... SITUATION DEVELOPING SWIFTLY TO EMBROIL ALL EUROPE....

Grimly Operator 5 passed the momentous strip of yellow to the ten uneasy men. "Gentlemen, the new World War has come!"

He peered into their appalled eyes, into their strained, white faces. He stood erect, eyes blazing through his black velvet mask, alert and commanding.

"Make your preparations immediately to return to your respective countries! Go with all possible haste! Warn your governments before it is too late!"

The shrill jangle of a telephone bell broke into the tense silence that followed. Z-7 whirled and strode again to the side of the room. He lifted a telephone from a table—an instrument connected with a secret wire—and when he brought the receiver to his ear he declared huskily: "WDC-13 is calling!"

Anxiously, the ten ministers without portfolio began to move toward the doors of the room. Operator 5 watched Z-7's gaunt face as the Washington Chief kept the receiver pressed hard. The black-eyed man straightened to say breathily:

"The President orders all known aliens to be arrested and jailed. It is our first move to keep us out of the new European conflict The spy menace is so great we dare not—"

A shock shook the room. A violent concussion trembled the walls, rattled the window-sashes, jarred the air. Through the curtains, a brilliant flare of light appeared, instantly to vanish. Like the reverberations of an earthquake, the tremor shuddered the foundations of the building; and from far away, from the very zenith, echoes rumbled back.

Z-7 tensely brought the transmitter close to his lips, "Where was that explosion?" he demanded breathlessly. "Where was it? *What?*"

His smouldering eyes rose to Operator 5's. His hands went white on the instrument. He stood transfixed, unable for a moment to repeat the words that had come screeching over the wire. His voice was a burst of breath.

"The Capitol has been bombed!"

At the side of the room, Operator 5 stood motionless. His eyes, midnight dark, peered toward the doors. They were closed. The ten unofficial ministers had gone. There was silence now within the four walls—silence until Jimmy Christopher's sharp words rang:

"The Secret League has struck the first blow!"

CHAPTER 4
DESTROYERS OF NATIONS

A PALL of terror enveloped the nation's capital.

Above the center of Washington hovered thinning mists borne on the night winds—vapors still rising from chaotic wreckage. Around the stricken Capitol building lay jumbled stone fallen from broken walls, spattered with glistening fragments of glass that had flown from burst windows. Black gaps were opened in the great gilt dome. Debris littered the majestic steps. Shrouded in acrid mists stood the damaged administrative building of the government of the United States.

Toward it Operator 5 drove in his Diesel-powered roadster while the paralytic shock of the explosion still stunned the city. The radiating avenues were filled with terrorized thousands, some fleeing the scene of destruction, some mobbing toward it. Cars choked the streets. Above the babble of hysterical voices rose the shrill screams of sirens. Clanging bells announced the approach of fire engines as the light of flames sparkled against the scarred facade of the Capitol. In the air, the tension of terror mounted higher and higher.

Jimmy Christopher left his roadster and grimly fought his way through the frenzied mobs, along sidewalks sprinkled with broken window panes. He had left the secret conference immediately the alarm had sounded, while Z-7 had hurried to Intelligence Headquarters. Now he reached a point close to the damaged building and gazed coldly upon it. Crowds jostled around him as he turned back. He shouldered through them to his roadster, slipped again behind the wheel, and started from the curb.

A flash of motion startled him. In the confusion of the crowd an arm was upthrown—a hand rose, gripping a glittering glass ball. Instantly it became a streak of light flashing through the air—a bolt of threatened danger striking toward Operator 5. He spurted his car in an effort to evade it. It hissed past his head. A muffled crash sounded. Instantly, inside the car, fire roared!

It snarled up swiftly. Flaming drops spattered, dashing upon Jimmy Christopher. The bright flare blinded him; intense heat stung his face and hands; a sharp pungency choked him. The instant the explosion struck he ceased breathing, in order to avoid drawing the flame into his nostrils; he made a swift move toward a fire extinguisher clipped under the dash. The roaring flame swelled savagely as he ducked from the door of the car.

Flames leaped up his coat as he turned the extinguisher-nozzle into the car. He was a figure of fire as the white stream shot out. Desperate, he jerked one arm from its sleeve, then the other, transferring the hissing instrument from stinging hand to stinging hand. The flaming garment dropped, and he leaped forward. He tore off his burning hat, whirled it away. Around him, startled cries sounded as he sprang close to the car, playing the whizzing stream upon the flames.

The splashing foam blotted blackness into the fire. Bit by bit, the fluid quenched the blaze as Jimmy Christopher swung the stream. Thick smoke billowed up as he drenched every square inch of leather and fabric. A morbidly curious crowd circled the car while he vanquished the flames. His darkened eyes swept from face to face in search of the man who had hurled the incendiary bomb, but the hunt was hopeless. He kept the extinguisher in his left hand; his right was ready for a quick draw of his arm-pitted automatic.

The last flicker of fire hissed out. Operator 5 continued to spray the interior while fumes gushed up, until the reservoir was empty, until the soaked seat ceased smoking. He ducked in

ANTON YUSSOV   LUTHER SIGMOND

SHEPARD HUNT

The
MASKED
POWER

CUPO   RAFFAELE CARRUCCI

again. He found the interior charred and soot-blackened, but
otherwise the car was unharmed. Had the bomb burst directly
upon him, he knew, he would have died almost instantly. Only
his alert move had saved him from a horrible death with seared
lungs and scorched eyes....

45

Gripping the wheel, forcing an opening through the crowd, he pulled away from the curb. Somewhere in the milling mob, he knew, was a man who had tried to murder him—a man who somehow had penetrated his cloak of secrecy and learned that he was Operator 5.

He drew to a stop in a quieter street, in front of a squalid restaurant. He turned his flashlight downward and discerned glittering fragments of glass—the broken shell of the bomb—lying on the blistered rubber mat. Drawing on gloves, he gathered them up, dropped them into an envelope. He left the car to enter the sordid restaurant.

He signaled his way past sentries, passed through secret doors, was lifted by a hidden elevator. He entered a suite of offices buzzing with activity. There was a constant clatter of teletype machines from the communications room. In an inner office, walled by file cabinets, Operator 5 knew that Z-7 was on duty. Here, so well hidden that lifelong residents of Washington might never suspect its existence, was the nerve center of the United States Intelligence Service. This was Headquarters WDC-13.

Operator 5 entered a spacious room devoted to fingerprint classification. It contained row upon row of cabinets containing millions of cards bearing the fingerprints of criminals, espionage agents, saboteurs, suspicious characters—a file greater even than that of the Bureau of Investigation of the Department of

Justice.* Operator 5 strode immediately to a table which bore equipment for the developing of latent fingerprints.

While the Intelligence experts assisted him, he applied liquids and powders to the fragments of broken glass he had brought from his roadster. He bent close grimly as smudges appeared, then clear-cut impressions. He jotted the classification of the prints on a card. Three men assisted him as he turned to the file cabinets. Within two minutes, Operator 5 found in a special file a set of prints corresponding to those on the fragments of glass.

He read from the entry quickly. "Shepard Hunt. American citizen. Radical agitator. Frequent arrests in New York. Whereabouts unknown...."

---

* AUTHOR'S NOTE: Except for this collection of the United States Intelligence Service, the collection of fingerprints of the Bureau of Investigation of the Department of Justice is the greatest in the world. It contains 4,320,000 sets of fingerprints (of which 750,000 are duplicates) and every day an average of 2,200 new sets are added as they are sent from police headquarters and other criminal investigation units in the United States. These are sent for identification, and a reply is wired back within thirty-six hours. Last year 3,818 fugitives from justice were detected by this means. The prints are filed according to the Henry System, devised by the late Sir ER. Henry of Scotland Yard, and to locate any one print among the millions on file takes only from three to ten minutes, except in the case of a loop print (300,000 of these are kept in a separate file) which takes an hour. Prints of 80,000 women are included. There is a separate file of 5,600 known kidnapers, bank robbers, extortionists and gangsters. This amazing selection is exceeded only by the files which Operator 5 is now consulting.

His eyes clouded, Operator 5 left the fingerprint room and strode to the door of an inner office.

Z-7 sprang to his feet as Jimmy Christopher entered. "New developments are coming at every moment! War is spreading over all of Europe like wildfire. Germany has just joined Balkaria with a declaration of war against Italy. France is expected to issue her declaration almost at once. Great Britain and Russia will be drawn into it before tomorrow passes. It is going to be a swift war—the most terrible the world has ever known!"

Operator 5's eyes narrowed. "Russia's entry into the war will be the signal for Japan to cross the Siberian border, Chief! When Russia is forced to throw her military strength west against Germany, Japan will take advantage of that fact to make her advance—to cripple Russian maneuvers in the East by seizing the Trans-Siberian Railway. Within a few hours this war will spread around the world—with the United States threatened both from the East and the West!"

Z-7's eyes blazed. "Japan, fighting Russia, will automatically be forced to ally herself with Germany. Our sympathies lie with Great Britain and France—our former allies. This, in turn, makes us the enemy of Japan! You are right: we stand between two fires!"

"At all costs, Chief," Jimmy Christopher cautioned, "we must keep out of this war. To enter it is to commit national suicide—to invite horrors far greater than those of the last World War. We shall soon see in use, Chief, more terrible weapons than have ever before been used—and worse, civilian populations, women and children, will perish by those weapons. Worst of all, perhaps, will be the widespread use of poison gas!" *

Z-7'S FIST thumped the desk. "You believe, Operator 5, that

---

* AUTHOR'S NOTE: The horrors of gas warfare were fully realized following the first World War. In his report to the Washington Naval Conference in 1922, General Pershing declared: "Chemical warfare should be abolished among nations as abhorrent to civilization. It is fraught with the gravest danger to non-combatants and demoralizes the better instincts of humanity." Yet the development of new poison gases has gone on apace.

Before the outbreak of the second World War, the Associated Press cabled from Paris, on Sept. 18, 1934, that the French newspaper *Le Jour* disclosed that day a method which makes poison gas deadly for eight days, perfected by German chemists. "A special, absorbent clay is impregnated with gases, then dried and sprayed from an airplane exhaust," the newspaper said. "Ground sprayed with this dust becomes an impregnable barrier, preventing not only the occupation of strategic territory, but making the evacuation of cities by civil populations impossible."

Shortly afterward, according to the Associated Press, one Philip del Fungo Giera, termed an international spy and the proprietor of a "mystery laboratory" near Monticello, disclosed that he had perfected a "sleeping gas," invisible and without odor, capable of felling a whole army within one minute.

At the meeting of the American Chemical Society in Cleveland last September, Professor H.S. Booth, head of the division of chemistry of the Cleveland College of Western Reserve University, announced the discovery of two new gases, *sulfuryl chlorofluoride* and *phosphoryl monochloro-difluoride*. Significantly the news account states that "both are highly irritating to the respiratory system." At the same meeting, Dr. George H. Cady of Clifton, the bombing of the Capitol tonight is an early move to hurl us into the European conflict?"

"I do! The explosion was timed to occur at the very moment when dispatches of the outbreak of the new war reached this country. It is a more daring piece of sabotage than the Black Tom disaster which shook all New York during the First World War. Never forget, Chief, that the Secret League, and the power behind it, wish to force us into the present war. They have already practiced sabotage in our navy—the sinking of the *Decatur*—and planned outrages that will arouse hysteria in the people of this country and force Congress to declare war on those we believe to be responsible."

"It is therefore of the highest importance that we prove these outrages are not blamed on any European nation—inform them that anti-nationalists are responsible," Z-7 said. "I have already

N.J., announced the discovery of a gas, a compound of *fluorine, oxygen* and *nitrogen,* "which is deadly poisonous and highly explosive."

According to Major General Amos A. Fries, chief of the U.S. Chemical Warfare Service, new poison gases have been invented fifty times superior to any known in the first World War and "the use of gas in that war was a child's game compared to what it will be in the future."

At the beginning of the first World War, 30 asphyxiating gases were known. Today there are more than 1,000. Poisonous gases can be manufactured speedily in chemical plants ordinary used for harmless preparations. Informed observers have declared that Germany, England, France and the United States are now able, in less than a week, to manufacture as much poison gas as was used during the whole first World War.

ordered every available man to investigate the bombing of the Capitol tonight. Are you quite sure that the Secret League is behind it? A false step now would be fatal."

Operator 5 nodded. "There is no link missing. First, the intercepted telegram to Yussov. Second, the fact that he is a physicist, possessing more technical knowledge than any other spy known to us, making it almost certain that he manufactured the counterfeit gyroscopes. I intend to prove that beyond all doubt. Last night I trailed Yussov for hours in an attempt to locate his laboratory, but he was shrewd enough not to go to it.

"Tonight, Chief, Tim Donovan is shadowing the exiled Balkarian. The man dares to show himself frequently, particularly at a certain restaurant where he appears every night. I sent Tim there immediately after we returned from the *Pennsylvania*. He's on the job now, and tonight I expect results."

"Tonight?" Z-7 queried.

"Tonight, Chief," Operator 5 answered. "Remember the intercepted telegram. The meeting of the Secret League was scheduled to take place exactly four weeks from the day it was sent. That is tonight!" Operator 5's fingers strayed unconsciously to his death's-head watch-charm. "In spite of anything that may happen, Chief, we must keep the United States out of the new World War. If we fail in that—"

He left unvoiced the dread that filled him. Quietly, he sat at his desk, took up reports that had been placed there. He read them rapidly, placing some aside.

Z-7 approached him with another. "When I got your report on Captain Macklin, I immediately started a thorough investigation of that man, Operator 5. He had been spending money liberally. There is no doubt that he was bribed to turn traitor by the Secret League. God—I hope that there are no others like him!"

Operator 5 turned darkened eyes. "We can expect to find others. We can expect the Secret League to strike again and again, Chief, until they force us into the war, or until we destroy them and the power behind them."

Z-7'S JAW clenched. "The world at war again—think of it! What can any nation gain by it? Millions will be slaughtered—it is beginning even now—and who will profit?" *

---

* AUTHOR'S NOTE: Reliable statistics declare that it cost approximately $25,000 to kill a man during the first World War. This figure is arrived at by dividing the total cost of the first World War (in the case of the United States alone, $39,158,649,009.57 to June 30, 1931, according to the report of the Secretary of the Treasury) by the number of casualties. Of this $25,000, it has been further stated, at least $10,000 found its way into the pockets of the armament manufacturers as profit.

Consider the following news dispatch of the International News Service, dated at Washington, Sept. 13, last:

"Seventeen million dollars in bonuses were paid to officers and high-salaried men from the huge wartime profits of the DuPont Company of Delaware, the Senate munitions committee was told today. Pierre S. DuPont, board chairman of the E.I. DuPont de Nemours Co., America's largest munitions company, furnished the bonus totals. He maintained that Europe and America demanded powder and war supplies, sales of which totaled one and one-quarter billion dollars."

"Who will profit?" Operator 5 turned sharply, and his voice took on an edge. "The sellers of machinery that kills! The makers of engines of slaughter! The manufacturers of armament will profit!"

Jimmy Christopher broke off suddenly as the door of the communications room snapped open. A shirt-sleeved man, face beaded with sweat, strode into the office carrying a teletype dispatch. He thrust it at Z-7 and exclaimed: "This has just come over the special wire from Mexico City!"

Operator 5's blue eyes sharpened at the message while the busy clatter from the communications room continued. Z-7 straightened tensely as he read:

> ... WDC-13... SECRET AGENTS OF BALKARIA KNOWN TO BE ACTIVE THROUGHOUT MEXICO... MEXICAN SECRET SERVICE OVERWHELMED BY THEIR NUMBERS... UNREST SPREADING AMONG ARMY... DANGEROUS REVOLUTIONISTS READY TO STRIKE AGAINST MEXICAN GOVERNMENT... REVOLUTION WILL SERIOUSLY ALTER INTERNATIONAL SITUATION... FERMENT DUE TO ACTIVITIES OF BALKARIAN AGITATORS... HINTS THAT REVOLUTIONISTS ARE SUPPLIED WITH ARMAMENT BY BALKARIA... FULL DETAILS FOLLOW... MCM....

Z-7 blanched. "Balkaria, even more militaristic than Germany, fomenting a revolution in Mexico! If that occurs—if the Balkarian agents gain control, it will bring an enemy to our very door!"

"Chief, the War Department must be informed of this at once!" Operator 5 exclaimed. "We must prepare against a possible outbreak of hostilities along the Mexican border. We are forewarned—we must make the most of it!"

Again an interruption came from the communications room. A telephone operator stepped through the door briskly. "Operator 5, a call for you on the Chief's wire! I do not recognize the voice, but the code word was given."

Jimmy Christopher swung to the telephone. At his quiet word, excited tones carried over the wire. "Tim, old boy!" Operator 5 exclaimed. "I've been waiting for word from you! Have you kept your man? Is he still—?"

Tim Donovan broke in breathlessly. "I haven't let him out of my sight a minute, Jimmy! Yussov doesn't know I've been watching him. He tried to throw off anybody that might be following, but I stuck."

"Good boy! Where is he now?"

A whispered address came over the line, and Jimmy Christopher jotted it down. "He may not stay long, Jimmy! I think he has an important engagement tonight. What shall I do?"

"Wait for me, Tim! I'm coming!"

Operator 5 broke the connection, rose quickly, and strode to the door of the inner office, pulling on his hat. Hand on the knob, he paused, looking back at the dismayed Z-7.

"Tim says that Yussov has an important engagement tonight,

Chief. It's the first meeting of the Secret League within the United States!" He strode out swiftly.

JIMMY CHRISTOPHER directed his Diesel-engined roadster around the hub of Washington, feeling acutely the tension of terror that tightened the air. Feverish activity was centered about the damaged Capitol. The fire corps, police and infantrymen were striving to hold back the stunned thousands crowding toward the scene. The radiating avenues had been roped off; army rifles glittered as sentries patrolled. Echoing the frantic note beating in every heart, newsboys shrilled from the street corners:

> France Wars on Balkaria and Germany!
> Russia Allies Herself With France!
> Attacks Expected in Saar Tomorrow!
> German Air Attacks Flay Italian Forces!
> Poland Issues Ultimatum to Russia!
> Great Britain's Declaration Expected!
> Capitol Bombing Laid to Balkaria!

The shouted words echoed mockingly in Jimmy Christopher's mind as he directed his roadster into a dark section of the city. He brought it to a stop in a squalid street that was odorous and deserted. He strode briskly past shabby tenements, toward the address Tim Donovan gave him. He noted, as he passed, the door bearing the number he sought. He walked more slowly until a whispered call, scarcely audible, reached his ears: "Jimmy!"

A quick step took Operator 5 toward a dark doorway. He melted into the shadow, came shoulder to shoulder with the boy

In thin, bony hands,
Yusov held a gyroscope.

A section of the room was revealed to Jimmy Christopher.

waiting there. Tim Donovan glanced furtively up and down the street to make certain no one else was near before he whispered: "Yussov went to the third floor, Jimmy. I saw the lights go on behind the curtains after he went in. He's still there."

"Good boy, Tim! I want you to stay here and watch that door. I'm going in."

"Alone?" the boy asked. "You're taking an awful chance!"

"I'm not going to try to capture Yussov, Tim. He's far more valuable to us free, at present, than if he were a prisoner. But he must be watched—never lost sight of for a moment. If he comes out before I get back—stick to his trail, Tim."

"Sure, Jimmy! But if you don't come back soon—?"

"Telephone Z-7 as soon as possible, the next address where Yussov goes. That's highly important. Now, old timer! Eyes sharp!"

Operator 5 stepped briskly from the doorway; Tim Donovan's gaze followed him anxiously. The boy watched him cross the street, approach the door which he had seen Anton Yussov enter. Filled with a growing concern, he saw Jimmy Christopher mount the steps and pause at the entrance. There was a moment of silence—and Tim Donovan realized, suddenly, that Operator 5 had vanished from the shadow.

Operator 5 stood erect in yellow gloom of a musty hallway, his back to the door through which he had passed. It had been locked, but he had drawn the bolt expertly with one of his master-keys.* Now he stood listening in the silence, peering through the glow of a single, dim bulb up an uncarpeted flight of stairs.

He trod up them carefully, testing each step, and came into another hallway. Again he climbed, to the third landing. "Yussov went to the third floor," Tim Donovan had declared and now, beneath the doors, Operator 5 saw bright light shining. Faint sounds of movement came from beyond. Jimmy Christopher, listening only a moment, turned to the flight which led to the fourth and top floor of the musty building.

Quietly he approached a door at the rear of the dark hallway. Finding it locked, he again brought his pack of master-keys into play. The simple lock opened at once. Jimmy Christopher opened the door into darkness, breathed rancid air which indicated that the rooms beyond had been long unoccupied. He crossed a bare floor to the rear window and looked down into a bleak court.

Silently, he raised the sash. Directly below, light was shining on the drawn blind of another window. Operator 5 looked around, found a chipped kitchen sink affixed to the wall, and stepped toward it. His nimble fingers reached into his left sleeve; he plucked at a hidden knot. He drew out the end of a thin silken rope, alive and supple, yet strong as steel.

He looped it about a faucet, uncoiled the full length from

---

* AUTHOR'S NOTE: These keys, as the followers of the adventures of Operator 5 already know, were fashioned by Jimmy Christopher in his work-shop and are capable of opening any existing type of lock.

his sleeve. Poising on the sill, he tested the strand and lowered himself. He descended hand over hand until he dangled outside the blinded window. He steadied himself on the sill, listened to the quiet sounds beyond the panes, and peered into a crack of light.

A SECTION of the room beyond was revealed to him—a corner filled with metal-working machinery. On the bed of a lathe, freshly cut chips of metal gleamed. Just inside the window sat a cluttered bench over which a shadow passed. A man stepped into view wearing a greasy smock. He was thin-faced, cold-eyed, bearded—Anton Yussov!

In thin, bony fingers Yussov held a shining metal instrument—a gyroscope. Grimly, Operator 5 watched as Yussov lowered it into a jar containing oil darkened by emery dust. The exiled Balkarian tightened the jar cap and, with painstaking care, affixed a seal with a counterfeit United States government stamp.

Operator 5's orders had kept the discovery of the defective gyroscopes and the capture of Captain Macklin a strict secret. From this laboratory had come the device responsible for the destruction of the *Decatur*. Anton Yussov stepped back and regarded, with evil satisfaction, an instrument capable of bringing disaster to another ship of the United States Navy.

Operator 5 watched grimly as Yussov glanced at a clock. The terrorist quickly threw off his smock, drew on a hat and coat. He turned toward the hallway door and opened it. Operator 5 hesitated; then, gripping the slender silken strand anew, he again lowered himself. He slid down until his feet touched the gritty ground of the yard; he sprang at once to the door which opened onto it.

Again a lock barred his way and again the old mechanism yielded at once to Jimmy Christopher's master-keys. He sidled into the yellow-lighted hallway as footfalls sounded on the stairs above. Anton Yussov was coming down. Operator 5 ran silently to the front entrance; he slipped through and closed the door as Yussov reached the first landing. He whirled, and long strides carried him across the street.

Tim Donovan gripped his arm. "Jimmy! Somebody else is watching this place!" the boy exclaimed. "He went past a few minutes ago, and around the corner! He might've seen you!"

"We'll have to chance that, Tim! Our man is on the move!"

Even as Operator 5 spoke, the entrance of the opposite building opened. At the head of the steps, Anton Yussov paused, as if waiting. Presently another man strode around the far corner and approached. Yussov descended; the two met on the sidewalk. They exchanged no word, but walked together rapidly. Operator 5 intently watched them as they turned from sight.

"Another member of the Secret League, Tim, without a doubt!"

He left the doorway and hurried through the shadows with the boy at his side. Reaching the corner, he paused in consternation. The sidewalk was empty. Yussov and his companion had disappeared! Operator 5 hesitated, his gaze centering on the broad, dimly lighted door of a garage, then turned back.

"Make it fast, Tim!"

He sprinted toward his roadster, and slipped behind the

wheel as Tim Donovan scrambled in beside him. The powerful engine hummed. Operator 5 sent the car spurting toward the corner. He passed the intersection and slowed, peering back. Out of the garage, he saw a cheap sedan roll and turn away. A flicker of light gave him a glimpse of the two men in its front seat. The man at the wheel was Yussov.

Operator 5 began a cautious, close chase of the sedan carrying the exiled Balkarian. It led him across Washington, past bright radiating avenues. It slowed at times, as though the men wished to listen to the howling of the newsboys running along the curbs.

> Poland and Hungary Join Conflict!
> Allies of Germany Mobilizing!
> Balkan Nations Issue Declarations!
> London in Terror of Enemy Air Raids!
> Japanese Moving Troops in East!
> War Sweeping All of Europe!

The shabby sedan penetrated into a dark, remote section of Washington and Operator 5 followed it warily. Abruptly it turned into a narrow street, slowing. Jimmy Christopher shot his roadster past the corner, leaped out and ran back, Tim Donovan close at his side. He peered into the lane of gloom.

The sedan had stopped. The two men were approaching the door of a house. Its windows were dark; they strode to a dark doorway. A faint shine of light shone as it opened and closed, as the two stepped inward.

Jimmy Christopher walked quietly along the opposite side of the street, eyes alert, Tim Donovan beside him. They swung suddenly through a gate and crouched behind a scraggly hedge. Silent, tense, they watched and saw several other dark figures move down the street, approach the dark door, and vanish through it. Other men came and vanished, and a period of silence followed. At last Operator 5 rose, and spoke in a whisper:

"The Secret League is in session!"

CHAPTER 5
THE HOODED POWER

OPERATOR 5 studied the dismal front of the house intently. Lightless, bleak, it appeared to be deserted, yet eleven men had entered its darkness. Somewhere behind its entrance, a momentous meeting was already taking place—a secret conclave of the most dangerous destructionists the world had ever known.

"Tim, your job is still to watch!" Operator 5 declared quietly. "Remember, if anything happens—if I shouldn't come back—you're to report to Z-7 as soon as possible."

The tough Irish lad watched anxiously as Jimmy Christopher stepped forward. Operator 5 was about to cross the sidewalk when a gleam of light appeared at the corner. Headlamps shafted over the pavement, and he whirled back. He ducked into the shadow again as a heavy, glittering car slowed and drew to the opposite curb.

A uniformed chauffeur slid from the wheel to open its door. From the tonneau, a huge man alighted, the high collar of a greatcoat shielding his face. He spoke a guttural word; he strode quickly to the entrance of the lightless house. His voice sounded low again; he passed inside.

Operator 5 rose after a moment. As he slowly crossed the street, he saw that the chauffeur was standing beside the car, waiting. He approached it silently, noting that its curtains were drawn. Light flared as the chauffeur lit a cigarette, and in the gleam Jimmy Christopher saw that the man's face was huge and square, powerful with a brutal ugliness.

Abruptly Operator 5 stepped into the open. Instantly the match flashed out and the chauffeur whirled to face him. The uniformed man's hand slid significantly into his pocket. Operator 5's lips tightened; his lips curved wryly.

"Who," he asked quietly, "is your employer?"

The chauffeur sneered. He growled: "Asking questions is dangerous!"

"Refusing to answer them," Operator 5 answered calmly, "is even more dangerous—to you. You are under arrest. You will—"

The big man lunged. His arm swung upward swiftly and a weighty automatic glittered in the light. The weapon slashed like black lightning toward Operator 5's head. Jimmy Christopher sidestepped nimbly. One hand shot out to grip the chauffeur's tendoned wrist; the other, flat and stiff, darted sharp fingertips to the side of the uniformed man's neck.

A burst of breath sounded. The big man stiffened, tottering on toe-tips. A swift wrench, and Jimmy Christopher tore the automatic from the man's numbed fingers. He whirled about, alertly glancing up and down the street as the chauffeur fell.

He gestured a quick signal to Tim Donovan to stay back, and he peered down grimly at the brute of a man on the sidewalk.

His jiu-jitsu blow, Operator 5 knew, would keep the chauffeur unconscious for several hours.*

Jimmy Christopher opened a front door of the sedan; he lifted the chauffeur with ease and deposited him on the cushion. He slipped his hand into a pocket of the car and brought out an envelope containing its registration papers. He glanced at the name on the blank—Martin Shelton—and his eyes grew puzzled. Closing the door and slipping the papers into his pocket, he entered the tonneau of the sedan.

A snap of a switch brought light. Installed on the seat was a dictaphone instrument, a wax cylinder on its drum. Black shreds upon the surface of the record indicated that it had been partly used. Jimmy Christopher quickly reset the needle and started the motor. Through the horn he heard a low voice speak gutturally—the voice of the man who had last entered the lightless house.

"Code H. Confidential instructions reaffirming previous orders. The outbreak of hostilities must in no way affect our policy. All payments must be made in gold before delivery. Governmental regulations will not deter us from adhering

---

* AUTHOR'S NOTE: Operator 5 trained in the science of jiu-jitsu in Tokyo under Kashawatska Hoia, who personally instructs the Heavenly Protectors or bodyguards of His Imperial Majesty the Emperor of Japan. He is also a graduate with honors of the world-famous *Salle d'Armes* of Scherevesky, who is master without peer of the fencing foils.

strictly to this demand. Only gold will be accepted, and gold received in payment is to be dispatched to my vaults immediately in accordance with previous instructions 5883."

A pause. Then again the low-toned voice resumed: "Code V. Imperative orders to all plants. Secret mines must be inspected hourly. Our most trusted men must be kept constantly on duty at the contacts. Any attempt at seizure of any plant by any government is the signal for its destruction. Our control must remain supreme. The penalty for failure is death—"

THERE THE voice broke off; the recording was at an end. The arrival of the sedan at the secret address had stopped the dictation. Operator 5 removed the wax cylinder and slipped it into his pocket, his eyes narrowed and sharp. He glanced about the tonneau and suddenly bent forward.

In the black leather which backed the front seat, the faint lines of a small door were visible—the opening of a compartment. Operator 5 removed from his pocket a slender steel tool and pried with it, but the compartment door was so closely fitted that he could not gain leverage. Again he brought out his master-keys; he inserted one after another into the lock. He worked intently, with grim concentration, on the most difficult mechanism he had ever tackled.

At last the click of the withdrawn bolt rewarded him. He lowered a leaf of metal and looked into a cavity with walls of welded steel. Inside were narrow pigeonholes filled with folded documents. Jimmy Christopher inspected them quickly and a chill gathered around his heart. He found countless communications couched in code, with translations of the ciphers clipped to them. The portent of the translations struck him with a dazing force.

They were reports of gigantic orders for armament filed by the governments now at war in Europe! They were a record of the grim preparations being made for a prolongation of the cataclysmic strife which even at that moment was rending a continent and threatening to embroil every nation on the face of the globe. Signed to the documents were the names of huge armament manufactories on the continent and in the United States.

In his hands Operator 5 held evidence of existence of a combine of makers of war supplies more gigantic and more powerful than a strife-torn world suspected!*

Operator 5 rolled the documents grimly, thrust them inside the dictagraph cylinder, and closed the compartment. He left the sedan quickly and faced the sinister house. Near the steps, he stooped to slip the momentous evidence into a dark cranny.

---

* AUTHOR'S NOTE: Startling revelations concerning the appalling worldwide ramifications of armament makers began to appear before a dismayed world almost a year before the outbreak of the second World War. It was disclosed that, beyond the shadow of a doubt, there was even then in Europe a huge, hidden force lying behind the arming and counterarming of nations. An international entanglement was disclosed; mines, smelters, armament works, holding companies, banks and political cliques, all working for the destruction of nationalism. It was revealed that the control of these companies was vested in not more than a handful of men whose power was known to reach above that of the state itself.

He passed to the side of the house and worked his way through deep darkness toward its rear.

He paused, facing a door set half below the level of the ground. He listened outside it, but could hear no sound. The way was barred. A moment's use of his master-keys convinced him that the door was not locked, but bolted. Again he brought out his thin, sharp-edged steel tool.

He inserted it into the crack of the door and probed until he found the bar. Levering it back and forth, thrusting it forward so that its sharp edge bit into the metal of the bolt, he worked the bar outward from its socket a minute fraction of an inch at a time. The process was soundless but torturously slow. At last, feeling the bolt loosen, he straightened. He eased the door open—and instantly he leaped back!

As a click sounded, spattering liquid fell from above the frame. It rained down past Operator 5's face as he recoiled. It brought a stinging pungency into the air, and as it struck the floor, a vicious sizzling sound followed. The viscid black stuff poured for long seconds, pooling just over the sill, and a thick white steam floated upward, chokingly thick.

Acid! The powerful reagent corroded the cement it struck, turned the wooden sill quickly into a charred, pulpy strip. Its action was instantaneous and continuous, a horrible, disintegrating force. Operator 5 backed from the fumes, recognizing the pungency of sulphuric and nitric acids combined electronically with a phosphoric compound. The trickling stuff glowed as it worked with an evil force.

Had not Operator 5 leaped backward at the first warning

click, the deadly stuff would have flowed over his body, quickly penetrating his clothing, blinding him, choking him, striking him down into an accumulating pool of doom, transforming him swiftly into a charred cadaver. He waited grimly until the stinging vapors wafted out of the air; then, tight-muscled, he moved forward again.

He sprang across the acid pool, into the darkness of the cellar. Making every move with the utmost care, lest he trip other traps, he moved to the base of a flight of stairs. At its top, he listened at a closed door. He opened it slowly, hearing a rumble of voices beyond, peering along a dark hall.

He stepped out, turned, and gazed upward along another flight down which the voices carried. He paused in the darkness as he heard a rustle of movement. Near the front entrance, a step sounded; against the frosted pane, a shadow appeared. A silhouetted man turned squarely to face along the hall, and his whispered question sounded: "Who's there?"

SWIFT STEPS carried Operator 5 forward. The shadow-man bent to peer as Jimmy Christopher passed through the dim gleam of the pane. A startled exclamation broke from his lips; he snatched an automatic from his pocket as he whirled. His hand shot toward a panel on the wall studded with push-buttons. His fingers spread over them as Operator 5 gripped his wrist.

They struggled savagely. Jimmy Christopher twisted his assailant's wrist violently and a moan of pain sounded. He struck the automatic down; he drove his fists hard into an evil, shining face. As the black man tottered against the wall, again frantically striving to reach the push-buttons, Operator 5 struck. His knuckles clicked against his adversary's spine, and a singing breath resulted.

Stiff as a statue, the shadow-man tottered, paralyzed in every muscle by the jiu-jitsu blow. Operator 5 caught him, lowered him. He rose, peering up the stairs, stepping close to the bank of buttons. That they were connected with alarm signals he could not doubt; that a touch upon them would have brought a murderous attack upon him was certain. Lips curved in a tight smile, he stepped across the man he had felled, to the base of the stairs.

Each step threatened the sounding of a signal, but Jimmy Christopher went up. No light shone in the upper hall save a line of light beneath a door, but the rumbling of voices was louder. Operator 5 shifted to another door at the rear. He entered a lightless room. He drifted to still another door communicating with the room where voices hummed. He listened there intently.

A shrill-voiced man was speaking. "It is inevitable! National lines began to disappear even before this declaration of war! Even Acting Premier Baldwin publicly admitted it!* Our mission is certain of success! We shall create upon this world one nation and one only!"

An excited chorus of assent followed. Into it broke a lower-

---

* AUTHOR'S NOTE: United States newspapers carried on August 4 last the following cable dispatch from London:

"A few days ago, Stanley Baldwin, Acting Premier, terminated a rather pedestrian speech in the House of Commons on the subject of increasing the toned voice, the same which Operator 5 had heard reproduced on the wax dictaphone cylinder. It spoke with authority, and immediately the room was stilled.

"Comrades, the greater part of our work is already done. War is raging in Europe. The United States will inevitably be drawn into it. It will become a new World War in every sense of the words. We then have only to wait, while every nation on the face of the earth destroys herself. We may stand and watch country after country disintegrate before our very eyes. We have done our work well!"

Another voice exclaimed: "It is only a question of days before the United States will be drawn into the conflict. Already the people and the press are beginning to clamor for action against Balkaria! They blame Balkaria for bombing the Capitol! I merit your congratulations, comrades, as a propagandist!"

Other voices rose. "Excellent work, Gavreau! You have made them believe it!" "We act, and Balkaria takes the blame!" "The United States is doomed!"

"Comrades!" a sharper voice stilled the others. "Listen to news I heard just before coming!" There was quiet again.

"The President has just called a special session of Congress! It is necessary because of the international situation! Some of

British Air Force with three sentences which perhaps are the most important spoken by any British statesman during the last decade. They were:

" 'When you think about the defense of England, you no longer think of the chalk cliffs of Dover. You think of the Rhine. That is where our frontier lies today!"

71

the people are already clamoring for war. Others are crying out against it—but war is on its way! A few words read in the Congressional Halls that have been demolished by bombs—by Balkaria, of course, comrades—a few strokes of the President's pen, and the United States will be at war!"

"Yes!" another cried. "This country will find it impossible to keep out! Even organizations created to insure peace must admit that!" *

AGAIN THE heavy voice spoke, stilling the others: "Brothers, the center of our activity must again turn to Europe. It is my plan to strengthen our organization there. From Balkaria I personally will direct our actions toward the goal. Success lies just ahead! You have worked well—your reward will come. In the meantime, I assure you of my continued support."

With the utmost care, Operator 5 tightened his fingers around the knob of the door. Without a sound, he eased it back until an infinitesimal crack appeared—until a thread of light fell across his face. He peered into the lighted room beyond, at

---

* AUTHOR'S NOTE: From a bulletin of the League of Nations Association of New York City concerning the Japanese situation: Answering the question, "What are the implications for the United States ?" this bulletin said:

"(a) That the threat of war anywhere in the world is of immediate and vital interest to the United States.

"(b) That it is infinitely better for the United States, in trying to prevent such a war, to act in coöperation with other nations. Isolated action is dangerous and ineffective. United action must be effective in the long run."

the man standing at the head of a table around which eleven others were seated.

The big man stood commandingly erect—masked! Over his head was drawn a cowl of black, and through narrow slits his steel-gray eyes glittered. His massive hands gestured emphatically as he spoke through the hood. Toward him the others faced, intent upon every word of their leader.

"You are loyal and unselfish, actuated by the highest ideals. You are remaking the history of the world. Posterity will hail you as among the greatest men who ever lived."

Operator 5's eyes grew dark. He eased back, and from a pocket of his coat whipped a velvet strip. He tightened it across his eyes, drew on black gloves. From his arm-pit holster he brought his automatic and leveled it. Again he reached for the knob of the door as he heard the heavy voice speaking again:

"Comrades, I bid you goodnight. I am leaving at once, as quickly as possible, for our new center of operations. Count the hours until triumph comes to us! Goodnight and—"

A swift step took Operator 5 through the door. He stopped with gun leveled at the hooded man at the farther end of the table. He saw the steel-gray eyes flicker; he saw the others in the room jerk in alarm. A sweep of his gun paralyzed them. His voice rang sharply into the stunned silence: "Not yet!"

His automatic trained steadily on the huge, hooded leader of the Secret League. While the galvanic tension continued he stepped forward, speaking ringingly again:

"You are not quite ready to leave this meeting, sir. Unless you wish me to shoot you down, you will remain exactly where you stand. Gentlemen—" His dark gaze flashed from face to face. "—remain seated as you are, and keep your hands in sight. The slightest move by any of you will invite a bullet."

Again, there was absolute silence, while the hooded man's gray eyes glittered dangerously—while the eleven sat paralyzed with shock. Operator 5 peered into their drawn faces, his lips curving wryly. His voice came level-toned, firm:

"You have listened to your leader. Now you will listen to me."

The cowled man leaned forward, pressing his huge hands flat to the tabletop. Huskily he demanded: "Who are you? Why have you come here? Do you realize that you will never live to leave this room?"

Operator 5 answered calmly: "I'll take my chances on that. I am here because I serve the United States, and you are her enemies. I promise you, gentlemen, the Secret League is doomed."

From the black hood came a throaty exclamation: "You are Operator 5!"

Operator 5's sharp gaze moved from face to face. "We're mutually acquainted. I recognize Monsieur Paul Gavreau, terrorist and propagandist, exiled from France. Next to him sits Anton Yussov, *saboteur*, expatriate of Balkaria. Between Italo Allegri, international criminal of Italian origin, and Peter Visian, political factionist of Austria, I see Mr. Wickham Seaton, a convicted and escaped traitor of Great Britain. I see Jan Rienze of Poland, Joseph Berh of Hungary, Luther Sigmond of Germany, and Hitsu Ataka of Japan. Herdet Rimar of Turkey is sitting, I regret to see, next to Mr. Shepard Hunt, a radical-minded citizen of the United States who has turned traitor to his country.

"All of you," Operator 5 went on grimly, "are sworn to the destruction of nations. But unwittingly, you are merely tools in the hands of your masked leader—tools he is using to achieve a colossally selfish purpose diametrically opposed to your ideals!"

THE STARTLED men at the table peered. The cowled leader remained bent forward, his great hands flattened on the tabletop. Operator 5 saw his steely eyes narrow dangerously.

"Dangerous though you men are to the existing order of nations," Jimmy Christopher continued firmly, "you are men of ideals. You are unselfishly striving to attain a utopian dream, destructive as your means of achieving it may be. I understand your motives, though I am emphatically unsympathetic. I again say that you are being deceived by your leader—that he has not disclosed his true purpose to you. Once you learn what it is, you will rebel against his leadership—and I am going to expose him here and now!"

The cowled man blurted huskily: "I warn you to be silent!"

Operator 5's smile tightened. "I take the liberty of disregarding your kind warning. It is my purpose to destroy the Secret League of Nations, and the truth will destroy it. Listen! Your leader, who keeps his face masked from you, is devoted to your ideals only insofar as they contribute to his own selfish ends. His aim is to destroy all existing nations and create one worldwide government only so that he may rule it—so that he alone may be Dictator of the World!"

The eyes of the eleven flashed toward the masked man. He

stood with head bowed, unmoving, eyes glinting. Into the startled silence, Operator 5 shouted again:

"This man wants war because, more than any other man living, he will profit from war. He is the controlling power in a gigantic combine of armament manufacturers. Into his pockets, even at this moment, are pouring vast fortunes in gold from national treasuries. His hands are grasping for the wealth of the world. He overshadows men like Zaharoff and Schneider.* He has already gone far toward attaining complete world dominion. Once he achieves his pinnacle of power, gentlemen, he will destroy you. He is your enemy as well as mine!"

Again the widened eyes of the eleven turned upon their masked leader. From the lips of Shepard Hunt, United States

---

* Author's Note: Sir Basil Zaharoff, called "a citizen of the world," and "the mystery man of Europe," established himself during the first World War as a master salesman of munitions and amassed a gigantic fortune. Of him, H.G. Wells wrote: "Indisputably this man has spent a large part of his life in the equipment and promotion of human slaughter."

Charles Prosper Eugéne Schneider is the executive head of hundreds of armament firms scattered throughout Europe. He is president of the Schneider-Creusot Company, the greatest of France's munitions makers. He is also president of the Union Européenne Industriale et Financiére, through which Schneider-Creusot controls 182 French companies which manufacture heavy ordnance, tanks, shells, ammunition, machine-guns and chemicals of warfare. Also, Schneider-Creusot controls 230 armament manufacturers *outside* France.

citizen in the Secret League, came a blurted question: "In God's name, is this true?"

Still the cowled man did not move. "He has no proof of what he says!"

"Gentlemen," Operator 5 declared, "I have proof—proof that will stagger the world when it becomes known. Obviously, since he has contributed great sums to your cause, your leader is a man of wealth. His money is tainted with human blood— profits from the making of engines of death.* He has financed the Secret League, not because he is an idealistic altruist, but because you have fomented war, and war means vast profits for him."

Again Shepard Hunt demanded of the masked man: "Is it true! Answer that question!"

Only the steely eyes of the cowled man spoke—threats directed at Operator 5.

"You know only too well, members of the Secret League," Jimmy Christopher continued, "the machinations of armament manufacturers. The fate of nations means nothing to them. All that counts is that nations fight and keep on fighting while fabulous profits pour into their pockets. They take no sides—

---

* AUTHOR'S NOTE: Statistics abundantly show the gigantic profits of firms engaged in the manufacture of armament. It is estimated that nations buy from Vickers-Armstrong, the great armament manufactory of England, war implements to the amount of about $100,000,000 yearly. This firm has, in fact, an agreement with the Sun Insurance Company whereby it is protected from making a profit of less than $4,500,000 a year!

they sell to all warring countries.* You know as well as I do the

* AUTHOR'S NOTE: During the first World War, British-made guns were used by the Germans to kill British soldiers, just as French armament firms furnished to Germany, through neutral intermediaries, materials for making explosives with which French soldiers were killed. During the recent invasion of Manchukuo, the Chinese forces used Japanese-made guns to kill Japanese infantrymen. Corroboration of these startling statements will be found in public utterances made by Rear Admiral Montagu William Warcop Peter Consett, British Naval Attaché. The practice continued unabated in Europe following the first World War. London lies at the mercy of air raiders from the continent and in this light the following dispatch, sent by cable to *The New York Times,* may be interesting:

"Copenhagen, Sept. 21.—The newspaper *Politiken* in a sensational front-page dispatch today charges the British with attempting to sell war-planes to Germany 'via Copenhagen.'

"Politiken says one of the outstanding exhibits of the recent international airplane show in Copenhagen was an Armstrong-Whitworth single-seater fighter ... said to be capable of 225 miles an hour. It was equipped with an Armstrong-Siddeley 640 horsepower engine and could reach an altitude of 2,000 meters in 3.5 minutes.

"The machine was inspected there, *Politiken* says, by the German government experts. Subsequently it was flown to Norway by a Captain Hughes ... and after a few hours was flown to Templehof Field, Berlin.

"Speaking of the Berlin visit, the newspaper reports: 'Here the European sales director for Armstrong, Captain Emery, who resides in Denmark, gave a demonstration before German authorities including Captain Christiansen, representative of General Goering.'"

details of the infamous Krupp-Vickers affair.* Explosives and steel have no loyalty! Before you, gentlemen, stands not a man, but an inhuman monster! I demand that you see his face!"

THE COWLED man stood unmoving. His eyes were bright metal behind the mask. He spoke slowly, into a strained silence: "One glance at my face will cost you your lives!"

Shepard Hunt's hands were curled into fists. "Remove your mask!" he demanded. "Let us see if that is proof of these statements! If we recognize you—"

"One moment!" The big man's voice thundered. "You wish proof? You do not need it—comrades!" The word rang with a sneer. "It is true that I have made you my tools—that I have blinded you with lies upholding your pretty ideals. I have used you—and I am done with you! War is here and the rest must follow. As for the charges made against me, I admit them!"

Dismayed, the members of the Secret League peered at the steel-gray eyes shining through the black cowl. "I no longer

---

* AUTHOR'S NOTE: During the first World War, German soldiers used Krupp hand-grenades fired by a patented detonator. This detonator was made use of by British manufacturers. It therefore followed that German soldiers were killed and maimed by hand grenades fired by a device originating in their own county. Even more startling, following the cessation of hostilities, Krupp sued the British firms for infringement of the patent, asking one shilling royalty for each Krupp fuse (KPz 96/04) used in the British hand grenades to kill German soldiers. The case was settled out of court for concessions valued at thirty million dollars. Thus Krupp collected royalties on a device used for killing soldiers of the Fatherland.

need your puny help!" the muffled voice rang. "Whole nations are aiding me now—destroying themselves in the fires of war! I do not fear the Secret League or any power that may be turned against me. My face? You wish to see it? You will never gaze at it! You want to know my name? You will never learn it! Because now—you die!"

His hand darted beneath the edge of the table. Instantly the room was filled with a sibilant hissing. Glances flashed upward, to the height of the walls, at a faint mist forming in the air under the ceiling. It was sizzling from pipes painted the color of the walls, through tiny holes—rushing into the air and vanishing as rapidly as it appeared. A touch of the masked man's hand on a lever concealed beneath the table had released the gas into the room. Now he straightened, his metallic eyes shining in merciless triumph, and repeated: "You die!"

Swiftly, three times, Operator 5 fired point-blank at the huge, masked figure. The cowled man jerked as the bullets struck his body. In his clothing, rips appeared where the slugs hit. But no blood flowed. Instead, through the gashes, shone the bright mesh of a bulletproof body-covering! Into the roar of Jimmy Christopher's gun, the huge man—suddenly, mockingly—laughed.

"Stop him!" Operator 5 snapped the command as the cowled man whirled toward the door behind him. The words rang through a scraping of chairs, the sound of sudden gasping, the continued hiss of the invisible gas. No odor was discernible in the air, yet the deadly power of the invisible fumes struck swiftly, devastatingly.

The eleven at the table sprang up, choking, coughing, moaning in torturous pain, clutching at their throats, staggering toward the doors. In their agony, their gasps for air brought only greater pain. They struggled blindly, groping, tongues protruding, seized by a lethal power that robbed them of strength even as they tried to escape.

The invisible fumes struck as swiftly at Operator 5 as at the others. His sight bleared; his lungs burned. His first breath of the deadly stuff urged another, and he fought to keep from drawing it. He exerted the utmost power of his will to prevent the powerful involuntary action of his lungs as he backed away.

Vaguely he heard a door slam, heard swift and heavy footfalls in the hallway. He leaped from the gas chamber and whirled away. Darting toward the hallway door of the rear room, he was shaken by a concussion that blasted out of the darkness—a thunderous roar, a blinding flash of light. He spun against the wall, breathing deeply of clean air, forcing his eyes to clear, and glimpsed a shadow of a man against the wall, crouching, gun leveled.

JIMMY CHRISTOPHER'S automatic swung up as the second shot cracked. Intense, stinging pain flashed into his right hand. His automatic spun away, clattering over the dark floor. He straightened, leaped sideward, snatching at the buckle of his belt. One swift movement brought into his hand the hilt of the rapier he wore sheathed in his belt, curled around his waist.

His arm flashed, and the flexible scabbard flew from the slender blade. He lunged, and his steel sparkled at the man tensing to fire a third time. The shot shook the room as blood gushed

Three times, swiftly, Operator 5 fired point-blank at the huge masked figure.

from the wound made by the rapier's razor edge. A snarl of rage sounded as the assailant sprang away. Operator 5 followed, blade twinkling, and the supple steel whipped upon the gun.

Like black magic, the weapon was torn from the killer's grip. Jimmy Christopher's blade flashed again as the other man sprang. He made no move—he crouched, hand raised, blade poised—but through the steel he felt a tremor. Its sharp point pierced with a hiss. Swiftly, then, Operator 5 recovered. An empty sigh sounded; the man in the shadow fell.

Operator 5 listened to a deathly silence. He swung to the door and snapped it open; he rushed to the front of the hallway. He jerked aside the blind of a window to peer into the street. No car was standing now at the curb in front of the house. Operator 5's enforced delay to defend himself against the gun attack had given the masked man a chance to escape. Filled with cold fury, Jimmy Christopher quickly turned back.

He strode into the rear room and his electric torch flashed. A circle of bright light played upon the face of the man who had died with the rapier run through his heart—Anton Yussov. Grimly Operator 5 strode back to the meeting room. From his pocket he brought a small silver case; from the case he removed two oval-shaped wafers of unglazed porcelain impregnated with a chemical compound. He inserted them into his nostrils, confident that they would counteract the effects of the deadly fumes.

The meeting place of the Secret League had become a room of death. On the floor men lay still and stiff, their faces contorted with horrible agony. The hissing of the gas had ceased—it had taken its toll with horrible swiftness. Thirteen live men had breathed in that room a few moments ago; nine dead men lay inside it now.

One of the Secret League had somehow managed to escape behind the cowled leader. Operator 5, glancing at the fearful faces of the dead, realized that that man was Shepard Hunt.

He turned from the room, leaving the door open, and quickly raised windows so that the gas would dissipate. He hurried down the stairs, removing the filters from his nostrils; he plunged into the cooler air of the street. His call carried softly into the quiet: "Tim!"

No voice answered him. No movement stirred the hedge behind which Jimmy Christopher had left the Irish lad. Operator 5 crossed the street hurriedly and stared into the blackness behind it—empty blackness. Chilled, dismayed, he peered up and down the dismal street and again he called.

"Tim! Tim!"

The name echoed emptily from the bleak fronts of the houses—echoed into a sinister silence....

CHAPTER 6
WAR FIRES BLAZE

IN THE inner office of Secret Intelligence headquarters WDC-13, the man known as Z-7 stood gaunt-faced, peering at sheaves of reports lying on his desk—reports from Intelligence agents scattered all over the world, information that was pouring into the Washington bureau by wire and radio. Frantic activity sounded within the communications room while shirt-sleeved men hurried to the Chief's desk carrying fresh dispatches.

The sudden opening of a door raised Z-7's eyes. Jimmy Christopher strode rapidly into the room. Before the Chief could speak, Operator 5 demanded tensely: "Chief, have you had any word from Tim?"

"Nothing!" Z-7 straightened grimly. "He has not communicated with this office. Why?"

Dark lines deepened around Jimmy Christopher's eyes. "God knows what's happened to him! Unless we hear from him soon, Chief, I'll—"

"Steady! I know what Tim means to you. We can only wait. Immediately you telephoned," Z-7 declared briskly, "I began following down the leads you uncovered. Our men are at Yussov's laboratory now, searching it. They may find no clues as to the power behind the Secret League, but no more defective gyroscopes will sink our ships—thanks to you! As for the masked leader of the League—the car in which be escaped was found abandoned a few minutes ago not far from the White House."

Operator 5 asked quickly: "Empty?"

"Empty, save for the dead chauffeur."

"Dead?" Jimmy Christopher exclaimed. "I left him unconscious, Chief, but—"

"He was dead," Z-7 insisted, "with a bullet through his head. Killed by the man he served, no doubt, to silence him! His identity will mean nothing to us now. The name under which the car was registered is a false one, and the address is also fictitious. We have been unable to locate Shepard Hunt so far, but we will not abandon that trail. He is the only known survivor of the Secret League. God! The man who used them as his tool is a merciless fiend!"

Operator 5 turned quickly to the reports on the desk. "The situation in Europe, Chief—?"

"It has assumed the gravest possible proportions. Read those reports. Great Britain has declared war! All minor European nations are mobilizing, and even the neutrals are frantically preparing to defend themselves against invasion. Germany is already massing her forces in the Saar. Even more alarming, the French line of underground fortresses is even now being attacked by rocket fire!" *

OPERATOR 5 was glancing quickly through the momentous reports. "England must throw up her defenses if she does not want to see London bombed off the face of the earth and

---

* Author's Note: Before the outbreak of the second World War, France took alarm at the discovery of a new weapon which she feared would be turned upon her, as the following' dispatch of the United Press testifies:

"PARIS.—Death rockets may win the next war, according to articles published in the French press.

"Following investigation of reports on German rearmament, certain French newspapers ... have begun a campaign to awaken the War and Air Ministries to the actual perils of Germany's warlike preparations.

"Special emphasis is placed on the construction of rocket bases in Germany, placed at an average of thirty kilometers from the frontier. One newspaper asserts it has definite information that Germany is constructing these bases

her ports destroyed with incendiary projectiles!* The Masked

of reinforced concrete from which projectiles called 'fusées' may be shot a distance of 200 kilometers.

"These projectiles can cover all strategic points, such as railroads, roads, stations, forts, and each fusée will have a destruction area of several thousand square meters.

"It is shown that if Germany should install such rocket bases from Belgium to Switzerland, making about 5,000 rocketguns in all, it would be possible to dump 50,000 tons of projectiles on France in a single night. This would represent for each base an average of ten tons per hour, comprising ten fusees of 100 kilograms, each, firing every six minutes.

"According to watchful newspapers nearer the Rhine, Germany is planning an altogether new kind of warfare for the future.... These newspapers assert that the so-called Maginot wall is perhaps invincible, and that the new Wrench fortifications may be unbreakable, but at the same time it is asked of what use will be the fortifications if all of France lies dead and burned behind them?"

* AUTHOR'S NOTE: Since the first World War, the size of air bombs has greatly increased. The largest bombs dropped on Paris and London weighed 660 pounds. Just before the outbreak of the second World War, ordnance experts were perfecting a bomb weighing two tons! One-ton bombs had come to be considered standard. The explosion of one of these, upon striking the grounds, is of sufficient power to make a crater sixty feet in diameter and twenty feet deep.

Incendiary bombs are even more damaging. Thermite, a mixture of aluminum powder and oxide of iron, fired by a primer when used in such bombs, creates such a terrifically high temperature that it will cause iron to melt and flow

Power has planned well, Chief. Unless this war is terminated soon, the whole world will be annihilated!"

From his pocket Jimmy Christopher brought the wax cylinder he had taken from the car of the Masked Power, and the document he had found in the steel compartment.

"There, Chief, is evidence that must be placed before every government of the world. Our one hope of bringing hostilities to an end is to prove to the people of the world that their governments have been tricked into fighting only for the sake of private profit."

Z-7 stared at the documents, and his haggard face went white. Operator 5 turned as the communications chief hurried from the adjoining room with a dispatch. He took it and read it rapidly:

…WDC-13…REVOLUTION MEXICO IMMINENT… CONCLUSIVE PROOF FOUND THAT OUTBREAK IS ENGINEERED BY BALKARIAN AGENTS…REVOLU- TIONISTS HAVE WEAPONS AT VALIENTE AND ARE PREPARED TO USE THEM AGAINST THE UNITED STATES… SITUATION GROWS GRAVER HOURLY… MCM….

Z-7's black eyes gleamed at the dispatch and he rose tensely. "The War Department is already concentrating on this situ-

---

as an incandescent liquid. It penetrates steel easily. A squadron of planes, dropping 100-pound thermite bombs on a city, is able to start so many raging fires that there can be no possible hope of controlling the destruction.

ation. Orders have gone out for a mobilization of our new tank units. At this very moment our new tanks—thousands of them—are being assembled and made ready against a possible invasion from the south!"

Another door of the office opened quickly. A young man wearing thick eyeglasses hurried to Z-7's desk carrying a sheaf of papers. Hurriedly he said: "Here's the translation of the latest cable message received from our agents in Balkaria, Chief. I will have the next for you in a moment."

Operator 5 leaned across the Washington Chief's shoulder to read the message as the youth returned to the Cipher Room.

WDC-13—Headquarters CB has again noted extraordinary transport movements. Mysterious shipments have been crossing the Balkarian border from the south and north. Labels on the heavy boxes indicate that they were dispatched from hostile as well as friendly nations. We know that these boxes have passed through shipping ports and across frontiers without inspection. They are closely guarded and moved hastily. Frequent shipments are received in Calkar and taken to a remote point outside die city. The circumstances are extremely suspicious; the nature of freight is unknown except that boxes are very strong and very heavy, though small.

Balkarian secret agents are watching all U.S. Intelligence operators here. It is certain they have discovered some of our most important lines of communication. Two of our men hove been arrested by the Balkarian secret police. Our activities are seriously restricted. At any moment we may be seized. Precautions being taken but danger growing hourly.—CB.

Operator 5's eyes grew dark as he studied the message. Z-7's knuckles rapped the desk anxiously. "Balkaria is in the very center of the theater of war, and we *must* have information from it. In view of the Mexican situation, the danger of our predicament would increase a thousandfold if our lines of communication were—"

AGAIN THE door slapped open, and again the bespectacled cipher expert hurried to the Chief's desk. He placed a typed sheet before Z-7 and blurted:

"Chief, this message does not decipher with any of our codes. The answer is that it is not a code at all—it is gibberish! Whatever information our Balkarian agents meant to send has been intercepted!"

"Intercepted!" Z-7 sprang to his feet. "That means the Balkarian secret police have closed down on our agents. They have seized our lines of communication!"

Operator 5 declared levelly: "That must be true of the cable dispatches, Chief, but the wireless station may still be operating. I suggest that you attempt to raise CB by air. It is absolutely imperative that our men in Calkar keep their messages coming!"

Z-7 strode into the clattering communications room and Operator 5 followed. Three men were on duty at sensitive wireless shortwave receivers. Into their earphones, messages were singing from scattered parts of the globe. Z-7's hand tightened on the shoulder of one of them.

"Call CB! Raise them as soon as possible!"

Z-7 waited tensely as the wireless operator adjusted his oscillator and threw switches. The sending key vibrated under the man's sensitive fingers. Through the ether flashed impulses seeking a sister station located far across the Atlantic, in the midst of war-torn Europe—a secret station maintained by U.S. Intelligence operators. Again and again the code call went out:

"Calling CB! Calling CB!"

After long, tense moments, the operator looked up to say: "There's no answer, Chief. I can't pick them up!"

"Keep trying!" And as the radio man turned again to his key, the Washington Chief blurted to Operator 5: "There is supposed to be a man on duty there twenty-four hours a day. God! If the Balkarian secret police have discovered that station, we are completely cut off from our men!"

Operator 5 turned quietly, and reentered the Chief's office. Again he studied the translated cable dispatch from Calkar; and suddenly he opened a huge metal file cabinet. From it he brought a folder of dispatches. He examined them quickly, and his dark gaze rose to Z-7's anxious face.

"Chief, the strange shipments reported by CB have been moving for some time. Here are reports that have come into this headquarters at intervals for months, giving information on similar unusual freight movements. All this extraordinary freight is flowing toward Calkar. It has come from every important capital. There is no record of its moving out again—it has gone to Calkar, and it is staying there. I believe, Chief, that pieced together, these reports reveal a vital part of the operations of the Masked Power."

"How?" Z-7 asked quickly.

"We know the plan of the Masked Power. He wants the warring nations to destroy themselves in the world conflict, and he is helping by supplying them with munitions. It is his intention to create a single state, after war has ceased, and to become the ruler of that state—the Dictator of the World! Until now, we have not known what weapon he is using to attain that dictatorship. It is—gold!"

"You believe these shipments—?"

"I have no proof, Chief. It is a theory—a strong one—which demands proof. But I believe the shipments mentioned in these reports are shipments of gold. The Masked Power, controlling a worldwide armament ring, is demanding gold in payment for the engines of war he sells. If I am right, these reports show that a steady stream of the precious metal is flowing from the treasuries of world powers into the vaults of the Masked Power.

"If this continues, Chief, he will in time control almost all the gold supply of the world! It will be a devastating financial power. He alone will remain strong after the nations of the world have toppled. Backed by the world's whole supply of gold, his control will be undeniable. For months this movement of gold to the vaults of the Masked Power has been taking place—and it is going on at this very hour!"

Z-7 STARED. "If that is true, the revelation of the truth will stagger the world. Nations will cease fighting because they *must* cease fighting to save themselves from annihilation. But before we dare to make that revelation, my boy, we must have absolute proof!"

"Exactly, Chief! It must be unquestionable!"

Z-7's fists bunched. "Proof—and how can we get it if our Intelligence agents in Balkaria have been discovered—if all our lines of communication have been cut off? If we cannot even reach our men, and instruct them to make the investigation—!" He whirled to the open door of the communications room and snapped at the anxious wireless operator: "Have you raised CB?"

"Not yet, Chief!"

"Keep trying to raise that station." He snatched up a blank, scribbled on it and flashed it toward men at another desk in the room. "Put that on the cables in Code R for CB! Make certain that it gets through! I've got to reach our men!"

Operator 5 faced Z-7 squarely as the Washington chief returned to his desk. "Chief, if we can't reach our agents in Balkaria, either by cable or by wireless, we will be forced to attempt to establish new lines of communication, no matter how desperate the effort!"

Z-7 nodded. "It is imperative!"

Another communications assistant stepped quickly through the door. "Special call on the Chief's wire!" he declared. "Message for Operator 5!"

Jimmy Christopher snatched up the telephone. His voice rang over the line and as the answer came, a vast sigh broke from him.

Tim Donovan's voice carried into the inner office. "Jimmy! This is the first chance I've had to phone you! I've been following the man in the mask!"

"Good boy! Are you all right? Where are you?"

"I'm calling from Bolling Field," the Irish lad responded.

"When I saw that masked man come out of the house and start off in the big car, I grabbed a chance and hung onto the trunk-rack. He changed into a taxi right away, and I got into another. He took a long time trying to throw off anybody that might be following—and then he headed for the field here.

"A plane was waiting for him—private cabin job. He hopped into it and it took off right away. He's heading for New York—I'm sure of that."

"Good work, Tim! Hold it!" Operator 5 turned to speak quickly to Z-7. "Chief, flash all airfields between here and New York to watch for a private cabin crate heading their way now. If it lands, the man in it is to be arrested on sight. Hurry it, Chief!"

As Z-7 hastened into the communications room, Operator 5 spoke gently to Tim Donovan. "Get right back to WDC-13."

A warm smile curved the lips of Jimmy Christopher as he turned from the instrument. Z-7 approached to say: "The alarm has gone out!" Operator 5 began to examine the reports on the table again, his eyes dark and thoughtful. He turned as fresh dispatches were brought from the communications room, and with Z-7 beside him he read them rapidly.

… NEW TANK UNITS BEING ASSEMBLED AND MOBILIZED… WAR DEPARTMENT MUST BE KEPT INFORMED OF ALL NEW DEVELOPMENTS IN MEXICO….

The name signed was that of the Chief of Staff of the United States Army and Navy. The second stated:

... WDC-13... BALKARIAN REVOLUTION-
ISTS IN MEXICO HAVE CENTERED ATTACK
AT VALIENTE... CERTAIN TO MOVE AGAINST
UNITED STATES... NOW AWAITING ORDERS
FROM BALKARIAN WAR OFFICE... SITUATION
EXTREMELY DANGEROUS... MCM....

Z-7's fist rapped the desk. "We must have word from those agents in Balkaria." He strode to the door of the communications room. "Roberts! Can't you raise CB?"

The wireless operator turned tensely from his dials. "No, sir! I can't raise them. There can be only one reason for that. The station is no longer operating."

Z-7 snapped, "Keep trying to raise it!" and turned to peer at Jimmy Christopher. "If the Balkarian secret police have discovered and destroyed that station, we are entirely cut off from our agents in Calkar!"

"And unless we learn the complete strategy behind the planned uprising in Mexico, Chief," Operator 5 declared in a low tone, "the United States will be forced into a war that will destroy her!"

CHAPTER 7
VOLUNTEER FOR DEATH

AN IMPECCABLY garbed young man approached the door of a staid apartment house in the East Sixties of Manhattan early the next evening. His Chesterfield was tailored to perfection; his silk hat sat on his head at a jaunty angle. He appeared carefree; only a few etched lines around his keen eyes evinced that grave responsibilities rested upon his square shoulders.

He was James Christopher, Operator 5, and as he approached the apartment-house entrance the doorman greeted him with "Good evening, Mr. Walsh."

Mr. Walsh ascended to the eleventh floor and, with a key of which no duplicate existed, unlocked a door built of steel and disguised with mahogany veneer. In a tasteful living room, he paused to read the headlines of the newspapers he had brought with him. Scareheads shouted their alarms:

Gas Bombs Dropped on London!
Paris Hit by Long-Range Shells!
Riots Against War Break Out in U.S.!
Government Seizes Broadcasting Chains!

And more startling:

People Demand U.S. Avenge Outrages!

Operator 5 examined the last paper minutely. It was the most famous daily in the United States, noted for its impartial reporting of world news; yet its front page reeked with propagandist appeals. Jimmy Christopher realized immediately that it was a forgery—a paper printed in a hidden plant by subversive terrorists, being sold to unsuspecting readers. It was another sly weapon in the hands of the Masked Power. He tossed the papers aside grimly and entered the adjoining bedroom.

There he swung toward the window a strange contrivance.

On an anchored table sat a huge drum; a cog cable connected a powerful electric motor with the drum, around which was coiled a rope ladder. On a flexible gooseneck, a small box like a camera poised, a lens on one side. Operator 5 opened the window, uncoiled forty feet of the ladder through it, and bent the gooseneck so that the box was thrust over the sill.

Calmly he legged out and descended into black space above a passageway far below. He swung when he reached the end of the ladder and sprang upon a balcony of the adjoining building. He brought a torch from his pocket and flashed its rays upward to the lens of the control unit of the mechanism. A photo-electric relay closed its contact; the rope ladder coiled upward and disappeared, and the window slid shut uncannily.

Operator 5 passed through another apartment and stepped into a hallway. He rounded a corner of the corridor and pressed a button inscribed: *Carleton Victor*.

A cool-faced manservant opened the door and greeted Operator 5 with "Good evening, Mr. Victor."

Crowe, gentleman's gentleman extraordinaire, did not suspect that Carleton Victor was a convenient cover under which Jimmy Christopher operated. Victor was a photographer whose reputation was worldwide, who maintained sumptuous studios on Fifth Avenue. World dignitaries, society leaders, industrial magnates, all sought the favor of his lens, for the signature of Victor on a photo-portrait was a credential of rare importance. None of his subjects dreamed, any more than did Crowe, that the great artist was in reality America's undercover ace.

CARLETON VICTOR allowed Crowe to take his coat, hat

and cane. He nodded agreeably when Crowe said, "Your dinner is served, sir." With an easy, "One moment, Crowe, please," he opened the door of a closet and stepped inside, closing it tightly.

The closet was soundproofed; it contained nothing but a telephone. It was an instrument used exclusively by Operator 5, and it was connected to a special secret wire. He called a number known only to a few select Intelligence operators and a voice answered: "Hotel Universale."

"Room 1313, please."

"We have no thirteenth floor."

"Room 1313, please," Operator 5 insisted.

Signals exchanged, he touched a cam in the wall which threw into the line a frequency-distorter that made eavesdropping impossible by transforming the low frequencies of the voice to high and the high to low, with the result that anyone listening in would hear only meaningless gibberish. At the other end of the line, a matched distorter reversed the process. A voice carried through clearly: "Z-7 speaking!"

"I've just come from dad's home, after leaving Roosevelt Field, Chief," Operator 5 reported. "Are there reports on the plane Tim spotted?"

"It has vanished!" the Washington Chief answered. "It landed at no known airport! The only possible conclusion is that the plane landed at some private field. I have ordered a close watch on all ships that have left or are about to leave New York."

"It's certain that the Masked Power is on his way to Balkaria even now, Chief," Jimmy Christopher answered. "But we have another important angle to tackle in the forged newspapers that are flooding the streets. We must do everything possible to fight that propaganda, Chief! The people must know the truth—that they are being forced into war by men who are thinking only of private profits. It must be impressed upon them that the truth has long been known.* Chief—has WDC-13 reached our wireless station at Calkar?"

"No! It is obvious now that the Balkarian secret police have cut off our communication with that country. We are still trying to reach Calkar, but I am afraid it is hopeless. Unless we get a break—"

"We will!" Operator 5 swore grimly. He racked the receiver, opened the door of the soundproofed closet. Carleton Victor stepped out. Crowe was waiting. He bowed and said, "Your dinner, sir," and Victor strode to an exquisitely appointed table placed in the sumptuous living room, near French windows which opened on a gardened terrace. He sat thoughtfully, looking about the room.

A dark glimmer came into his eyes. When Crowe approached, he asked quietly: "You were out of the penthouse a short time, a little while ago, Crowe?"

"Yes, sir. To select the chops, sir."

"Crowe, I wish you would step into the closet of the bedroom and count the number of pairs of my shoes in the rack."

"Yes, sir? Of course, sir!"

Crowe turned away bewildered, and Carleton Victor

---

* AUTHOR'S NOTE: "We all know that this was a commercial war!" Woodrow Wilson said in a speech at St. Louis, September 5, 1919.

neglected the soup. The manservant returned, still puzzled, with his report.

"There are twenty pairs, sir."

"And how many do I have, Crowe?"

"Twenty-one, sir. Including, of course, sir, the pair you are wearing."

"Then, Crowe," Victor said, his lips tightening, "you haven't become so careless as to leave any of my shoes in odd places?"

"No, sir! I don't understand, sir!"

Victor straightened. "Suppose," he said, "you lay another place at the table, Crowe. This will be a dinner for two. We have a guest."

"A guest? Yes, sir! At once, sir!"

Again the manservant, blinking confusedly, hurried away. Carleton Victor still left his soup untasted. He reached inside his dinner coat and removed a small, polished automatic He rose, leveling it across the room. When he spoke, he said very quietly: "Please take a chair, sir. Crowe becomes quite distressed when he has to wait dinner."

Silence followed. Carleton Victor's gaze lowered to the bottom of the heavy window drape. Beneath its edge, unnoticeable except to one whose eyes were as sharp as Carleton Victor's, the toe of a man's shoe was visible. The silence continued until Victor said: "Come—don't delay Crowe's dinner!"

A SHARP movement ruffled the drapes. It was the raising of an arm, a desperate gesture by a man hidden behind it. It meant that a hand was slipping toward a gun. The movement jerked to a stop as Victor's voice rang.

"And behave, please, in a manner becoming a guest!"

He stepped forward. His automatic leveled as he gripped the drape and snapped it aside. The light revealed a white-faced man pressed to the wall, his eyes shining with alarm, his hand thrust under his coat. Victor's quick move reached beyond that hand; when he stepped back, he was holding two automatics.

"Good evening, Mr. Shepard Hunt!" he said very quietly.

The man at the wall did not move. The face was grayed, the eyes grim. Carleton Victor's hands darted over his pockets in search of another weapon; discovering none, Victor stepped back and lowered his gun.

"An unexpected pleasure," he said, grimly. "My compliments, Mr. Hunt. No doubt you have had me under observation for a long time. You have discovered a fact which is known to only five people in the world. That many and no more know that Carleton Victor is something other than a photographer."

Shepard Hunt peered intently into Victor's eyes and did not speak.

"You came here tonight, of course," Victor said, "slipping in while Crowe was out, for the purpose of murdering me."

Hunt blurted: "I know the penalty for turning traitor in time of war! You intend for me to suffer it!"

Carleton Victor smiled slowly. "Mr. Hunt, my intentions are often surprising. I was distressed to find a citizen of the United States acting as a member of the Secret League—especially a man of your caliber. You see, I know something about you. You are a courageous man, if a dangerous one; you are shrewd and capable. I have regretted, Mr. Hunt, that you were devoting yourself to the destruction of your country instead of its preservation."

Hunt straightened. "I was a soldier, sir. I fought in France. I know the horrors of war. I know that wars are fomented by selfish interests. My ideal is to stop the horror of it by helping to create a single state in which war is impossible. If hating human slaughter is treason, sir, I am guilty of treason!"

Again Carleton Victor's lips tightened. "Odd!" he said quietly. "I agree with you completely. You and I have been working against each other, and yet our purposes are the same—to save the world from the ravages of war. Unfortunately, you have been misled—duped by a man whose power comes from the spilling of blood. If he ever gets complete rule of the world, he will hold it by two means—gold and arms. Will the single state put an end to war? No! It will mean a continuous, despotic war such as the world has never seen before!"

Shepard Hunt shrugged. "I know. I've been a fool. Well, you've got me—I'll face the consequences. I'm ready to accept them."

Carleton Victor smiled. He turned to a luxurious divan and placed the two automatics under a cushion. He faced the man who alone survived the Secret League.

"Instead," he said, "let's have dinner together."

Amazement filled Hunt's eyes. Crowe hurried into the room and hastily laid a second place at the table. Victor gestured Hunt to a chair. The bewildered man took it uncertainly; across spotless linen and exquisite silver and crystal, he faced the man who possessed the power to doom him to death. Victor's manner became genial and suave; and they ate.

VICTOR SAID quietly, as the manservant served the coffee, "We are not to be disturbed, Crowe." He offered Hunt a cigarette from a gold case. Through clouds of smoke, they regarded each other. Victor began to speak in a firm, level tone.

"Now let's talk this over. Let's consider the men who make armaments, and the power they wield. Let me refresh your memory on two of the most startling examples of how those who trade in death work!

"The greatest of France's munitions makers, Schneider-Creusot, helped arm France during the World War—as well as France's enemies! When the time came for governments to pay their bills, firms like Schneider-Creusot and Vickers were always, somehow, first in line. Many a bond issue was floated in Europe for no other reason than that the sellers of slaughtering machines might be paid. And when the First World War stopped, Schneider-Creusot continued to sell arms and, since France needed less than before, found business elsewhere.

"Hungary, an enemy of France during that war, then potentially an enemy in the future, was forbidden by the Treaty of Trianon to arm—but Schneider-Creusot filled its orders for munitions gladly. When the time came for Hungary to pay the bills, Mr. Hunt, Hungary couldn't pay. What could be done? The armament manufacturers supplied the answer.

"The French government loaned the money to Hungary! Hungary paid Schneider-Creusot! The result? The French taxpayers paid the bills for equipping 300,000 soldiers of an enemy power! That army, Mr. Hunt, is at this very moment fighting France with that selfsame armament!"

Shepard Hunt listened intently.

"As for the second instance, it is even more appalling," Carleton Victor continued. "It means that millions of men died needlessly, that every American who perished in the First World War need not have died! Every soldier, Allied and German alike, who was killed between the spring of 1917 and November 11, 1918, was needlessly slaughtered! The First World War would have ended before America entered it if it had not been for the makers of war-engines!

"Early in the First World War, the German advance wrested from France the control of the Briey basin. Before that time the Briey basin had supplied France with seventy per cent of the ore she used. After the seizure, the mines were operated for the benefit of Germany. They supplied her with almost three-quarters of the ore she consumed during the war. After two years, the advance of the French army brought it close to Briey. During the second battle of Verdun, Briey lay within range of the Second French Army and only twenty-five miles from an American training sector.

"The Briey mines and smelters were turning out tons of raw materials every day which were being turned into weapons of death and used to mow down French troops. The very heart of the German source of war materials was within easy reach of the French air forces. Yet, did those air forces bomb the Briey mines and smelters out of existence in what would have been a telling, decisive blow against Germany? Was the blow delivered which would have ended the war?

"No! The huge works remained untouched! Why? French

General Headquarters explained that if they destroyed Briey, Germany would retaliate by destroying Dombasle, between the Argonne and Verdun, which was supplying the French with raw materials for war! So both sources continued to pour out their weapons of destruction and millions were needlessly killed. The war might have ended then and there—but so would the war profits! That was why Briey and Dombasle came through the war unscathed—why American troops were sacrificed to the merchants of death!" *

Shepard Hunt was gazing at Carleton Victor with fascination now, as the latter talked. There was horror in Hunt's eyes.

"These practices, Mr. Hunt," Victor went on, "continued up to the outbreak of the Second World War. God forbid that we enter it, but if we do, we must face enemies whom we have helped arm!**

* AUTHOR'S NOTE: Operator 5 has here stated only accepted facts.

** AUTHOR'S NOTE: "NAZIS CHARGED WITH BUYING ARMS IN U.S.

"PARIS, Sept 11.—The charge that a mysterious syndicate bought more than $5,000,000 worth of arms and ammunition from American munitions manufacturers and shipped them to Germany this year was made to International News Service today by a well-informed foreign diplomat.

"Captain Ernst Roehm, General Kurt von Schleicher and others executed during Hitler's famous 'blood bath' last June were put to death because they diverted part of the shipments to their use.

"The arms, which included machine guns, bombs, rifles, pistols, airplane motors and ammunition, were intended for use in Austria and Czechoslo-

"Even at this moment, in Europe, armament manufacturers are supplying munitions to the enemies of their governments for the destruction of soldiers of their own country.* It is into

vakia, the diplomat said, and the Italian and Austrian governments knew of the shipments."

This news dispatch was published in the United States on the date stated above.

* AUTHOR'S NOTE: Operator 5 is here referring to facts disclosed before the outbreak of the second World War, of which the following are a few of the most significant.

General Sir Herbert A. Lawrence, chairman of the British armament firm of Vickers, Ltd., at the annual meeting of the Vickers shareholders on March 26, 1934, when asked if Vickers was assisting in the rearmament of Germany, then Britain's potential enemy, answered that he could not give any assurance in definite terms—he was unable to deny it!

M. Faure, speaking in the French Chamber of Deputies on February 11, 1932, implied that French money was being directed subversively into the campaign fund of Hitler when he declared:

"It is a fact that the directors of Skoda, which is controlled by Schnei-der-Creusot, have supported the election campaign of Hitler."

The Dutch paper, *Freie Presse*, published at Amsterdam, printed on August 26, 1933, a report that Schneider-Creusot had delivered 500 tanks to Germany in violation of the Versailles Treaty. Though the report was widely reprinted, it was never refuted. When, on October 4, 1933, M. Senac, executive member of the French Association of War Veterans, declared that Schneider-Creusot had delivered 400 more tanks to Germany, he demanded an investigation. So far as can be determined, no investigation was made. It this horrible, merciless, inhuman mêlée that the United States is being forced!"

SHEPARD HUNT'S eyes blazed. "You've convinced me! And you fill me with shame that I allowed myself to become a tool of the steel monsters. If I could wipe away what I have done—but now it is too late."

Carleton Victor declared quietly: "No, it is not too late!" He leaned forward intently. "You are my prisoner. The penalty for your actions is death. You are a man I should not wish to see die in dishonor. On my own responsibility, Mr. Hunt, I offer you an opportunity to serve your country."

Hunt started. "In God's name, what do you mean?"

"I ask you to stand shoulder to shoulder with me, to devote yourself to the destruction of the Masked Power, to attempt

---

was known that prominent French officials, including former Presidents of France, were at the time directors of subsidiaries of the Comité des Forges de France, of which association Schneider-Creusot and other munitions makers are members. Francois de Weudel, head of the comité, is a member of the House of Deputies of France, the owner of a string of influential newspapers, regent of the Bank of France and a strong political figure. The answer to the question why France continued to arm her potential enemy must, the world justifiably assumed, lie in those facts.

Finally, as an illustration of the attitude of the makers of war engines, this statement is significant. The head of the Hirtenberger Munitions Fabriken of Austria, Herr Mandl, when asked if he was not aware that his exports of war materials to Germany violated international agreements, answered: "I sell arms and munitions. It is not my business to interpret treaties."

to annihilate the munitions combine. I warn you, it may mean death. It means playing a million-to-one chance. I cannot offer you immunity, because that is beyond my power—I cannot even help you if another Intelligence Operator should take you prisoner. But I will allow you to go free in return for your promise to fight the Masked Power—your word of honor."

For a long moment Shepard Hunt was silent, his eyes glinting, his lips curving sourly. "My word of honor," he repeated slowly. "Has a traitor—?"

"Yes!" Carleton Victor said. "You have! In return, I pledge myself to do everything possible to help you. I may be able to accomplish nothing—but I will try. A bargain, Mr. Hunt. An agreement between gentlemen. Do you accept it?"

"I accept it!"

Their hands clasped above the table, and they peered deeply into each other's eyes during a moment of silence. Carleton Victor rose. He strode to the divan, removed the larger automatic from beneath the cushion, and extended it to Hunt. Hunt's fingers closed about the butt slowly, his eyes still on Victor's. Victor stood unmoving as Hunt's finger curled into the trigger.

"One pull upon it," Victor said softly, "and you can escape. You can slip out of the country. You can evade entirely the consequences of treason. One shot—"

"I have given my word of honor!" The gun disappeared inside Hunt's coat. Victor smiled slowly.

"Good!" he said. "You have been close to the Masked Power,

Mr. Hunt. Where is he? Who is he? When he is in this country, where does he hide?"

Hunt's face twisted. "I don't know who he is! I have never seen him without the mask. By now, he has left the country—on his way to Balkaria—but I cannot be more definite. If I saw him again, though I've never seen his face, I would recognize him—his voice, his walk, his build, but—"

"You," Carleton Victor declared, "are to watch for that man. He is certain to return to this country. You, and no other man living, will be able to spot him. Night and day you are to do everything possible to find him. If you do, I want your report."

Hunt said firmly: "You shall have it!"

"I repeat—it is dangerous. That man is closely guarded, and he has taken extraordinary precautions to protect himself. He may know that you have survived the Secret League—even now he may be seeking to silence you. But your orders are: Find him!"

"I'll find him!" Shepard made the declaration grimly. Carleton Victor turned to the door and Hunt followed.

"Your address, Mr. Hunt?"

"The Fairlee Hotel, Room 1040."

The door opened; but Hunt paused, peering into Victor's eyes. "God! Disloyalty is impossible to a man like you, sir."

He strode away with quick steps. Carleton Victor quietly closed the door and called Crowe. The manservant appeared, helped him with coat and hat. Victor stepped to the entrance, pulling on his gloves, his gleaming cane tucked under his arm.

"The dinner, sir?" Crowe ventured. "Was it satisfactory?"

"It was quite the best dinner, Crowe," Carleton Victor

answered, "I have ever had with a man whose first intention was to murder me."

He stepped out the door and left the manservant staring at the panels in abject dismay.

CHAPTER 8
MENACE IN THE SOUTH

OPERATOR 5 left a taxi in front of a modest brownstone house in the East Forties of New York. On the street corners, newsboys were screeching the headlines of the latest editions to pour from constantly thundering newspaper presses. He paused and listened intently:

German Troops Advancing in Saar!
Air Raid Repulsed Over Paris!
Mass Meetings in U.S. Advocate War!
Declaration by U.S. Inevitable!
Rioting in Big Cities!
More Outrages Feared!

Jimmy Christopher strode grimly to the entrance of the house and admitted himself with a key. Quick steps sounded on the stairs as he approached them. Tim Donovan bounded from the living room, grinning broadly.

"Gee, Jimmy, I'm sure glad you've come! Di's here, and Dad. We've been talking about the United States declaring war. Do you think we will?"

"I'll do everything I can to prevent it, Tim," Operator 5

declared as he strode up the stairs with the boy. "It would be fatal. We've got to keep out of it!"

Operator 5 strode into the living room as a girl hurried toward him. She was in her early twenties and exceedingly pretty—alert, vivacious, with eyes that bespoke a wisdom beyond her age. She flung her arms around Jimmy Christopher's neck and kissed his lips. He backed away laughing, his face colored.

"Lord, Di! Are you that glad to see me?"

Diane Elliot echoed his laughter. "I'm always gladder to see you than anyone else alive, Jimmy Christopher!" she declared. "You're always so busy that I scarcely get a glimpse of you!"

She kept his hand in hers as he turned to greet the mild-mannered man who rose from a chair, smiling and with hand extended. Diane Elliot, in spite of her youthfulness, had achieved distinction in newspaper work and held a position of responsibility with the worldwide Amalgamated Press news service. In the past, she had assisted Operator 5 on important cases while respecting his necessity of secrecy though she burned to publish the facts he disclosed to her. She stood beside him proudly now as Jimmy Christopher greeted the man who had once been Operator Q-6 in the United States Intelligence.

"Glad to see you again, Dad!" he exclaimed to John Christopher. "Lord, it's so pleasant and peaceful here it's hard to imagine that a war is being fought. Has Z-7 called, Dad?"

"No, my boy," ex-Operator Q-6 answered.

Jimmy Christopher turned to gaze at Diane. "Di, are you busy? Can you handle a job for me—a job that's highly important, that I can't risk giving to one of our agents?"

"Just tell me what it is, Jimmy!" Diane exclaimed. "I'll show you!"

"At the Hotel Fairlee, in Room 1040, lives a man named Shepard Hunt. He is a fugitive. I want you to watch him. It's not what you think, Di—I don't want him, because he's working with me. But that man is in grave danger. He's undertaken an extremely hazardous job, and he must be kept in sight every hour out of the twenty-four.

"I want you and Dad to relieve each other at the task of watching him. One of our regular inspectors might be spotted, but you stand a better chance. If any attempt is made on his life, it is of the utmost importance to find out who is responsible. Will you do it, Di? Dad?"

"I certainly will, Jimmy!" the girl declared.

John Christopher's eyes glittered. "Son, I welcome a chance to do something for the Service. I'm tired of taking care of myself and tired of doctor's orders. Nothing will please me better than to get into action again!"

JOHN CHRISTOPHER had been forced to retire from the service when seriously wounded. Two bullets, lodged so close to his heart that no surgeon dared operate, continually threatened his life. He had been warned against undue exertion, for death might strike him down at any moment. At Operator 5's suggestion, he had become alert, zestful.

"Di, I'll take the first trick!" the older man declared. "I'll phone you when to relieve me." He drew on his hat and coat, gazing at Operator 5 fondly. "I'm proud to help, son!"

"Nonsense, Dad! I can never hope to equal you. Go to it—

but watch sharp. If Hunt is attacked, remember, spot the men responsible. It will be a lead of the highest importance!"

"I'm on my way!" John Christopher hurried down the stairway, and the entrance clicked. Operator 5 was silent. Tim Donovan came toward him eagerly, burning with something to say.

"Jimmy, you've shown me lots of swell tricks—and this time I'm going to show you one! I worked it out, and it's going to fool you."

"Turnabout's fair play. I'm prepared to be completely baffled."

The boy brought from his pocket three ordinary packets of matches. He opened them, disclosed that each contained the usual twenty matches. Closing them again, he placed them side by side on the table.

"Now, Jimmy, I'm going to show you how I can detect a very slight change in weight of one of those folders of matches—the weight of just one match. I'm going to go out of the room and while I can't see you, I want you to pick up one of those packets, tear just one match from it, close the folder, and put it back."

"Okay, Tim. Out you go!"

The Irish lad hurried from the room and closed the door. Smiling, while Diane watched, Operator 5 took up one of the folders and followed directions by removing only one match from it. He replaced it in exactly the same position on the table and when he called, Tim bounded in.

The boy became very solemn over the problem. He picked up two of the packets, one in each hand, and appeared to weigh them. He replaced one, took up the third, and again seemed to judge their relative weight without glancing at them. Then, quickly, he tossed the others aside and held up the third.

"That's the one, Jimmy!"

"Right, Tim! You've fooled me completely. You didn't really tell which one it was by the weight alone, did you?"

"Naw, Jimmy—it's a trick!" the boy exclaimed. "Anybody can do it. You see, when I opened the folders to show you the matches, I gave the flap of each one a slight twist to one side. When I closed the folders, I made sure that each flap was tucked in so that it was just even with the bottom on both sides. All of them were the same. But when you opened one of the packets to tear out a match, and then closed it, the twist I'd given to the flap made it protrude a little on one side. I only pretended to weigh the folders. I knew right away it was the one with the flap that wasn't quite in place."

"That's a slick one, Tim," Jimmy Christopher complimented the boy, as Diane laughed at the simplicity of it. "Now suppose I show you one. Wait here, and I promise you'll be completely deceived."

THE IRISH lad waited eagerly while Operator 5 stepped through a door at the rear, into his workshop. The rooms beyond were equipped with woodworking machinery, an electric bench, a small chemical laboratory, and on the shelves were stored strange devices the nature of which were known only to Operator 5. It was here that he devised and perfected his feats of legerdemain. When he returned, however, the objects he brought were not in any way mysterious.

"This is an ordinary egg-cup, Tim, as you see. This is a small block of iron that I will use as an anvil. Here are a small hammer, a buttonhook, and a pistol. It's a blank pistol, but even a cap-gun would do, because of the magical forces I will call into play. Now, Tim, please lend me your ring."

The boy removed from his finger the ring with its skull and mystic numeral 5 which Operator 5 had given him. Jimmy Christopher returned to the table, picked up the hammer, placed the ring on the block of metal—and began to pound on it.

"Don't do that!" the startled boy exclaimed. "Gee, you're smashing it! Jimmy—my ring!"

"Worried, Tim?" Operator 5 inquired calmly as he continued to hammer. "I've got to smash it in order to get it into the gun." He hammered still harder while the boy peered in dismay. "There—it's almost flattened out! I think it will fit now." He tried to force the misshapen bit of metal into the bore of the pistol and, finding it would not enter, hammered vigorously again, while Tim watched in anxiety. "This time—yes, it goes in!"

He dropped the beaten metal into the gun barrel, wadded a small piece of paper, and thrust the wad after it. Then, putting the pistol aside on the table, he took up the egg-cup and showed Tim that it was empty.

"Now," he directed, "go to the refrigerator, Tim, and bring me an egg."

The boy hurried into the kitchen. Diane Elliot smiled anxiously. "Jimmy, you've almost broken his heart. His ring is the most precious thing in the world to him!"

As Tim hurried back, Operator 5 answered with a solemn wag of his head, "Then I'll certainly have to restore it, Di!"

"A fresh egg right out of the box," he went on, taking it. "Very well, Tim—now watch! I place the egg in the egg-cup—so! I put the cup containing the egg here on the table. I take up the pistol, aim at the egg, invoke the powers of magic and—"

A sharp report sounded as the gun exploded. Jimmy Christopher again laid it aside. He took up the small hammer and, tapping gently, cracked the top of the eggshell. Then, with the buttonhook, he probed into the egg, his face very solemn.

"Unless the powers of magic have failed me, Tim, the ring should now be completely restored and inside this egg. But I haven't found it yet. One moment, Tim. There! I've got it! There's the ring!"

Jimmy Christopher pulled the buttonhook from the inside of the egg—and hanging to it was Tim Donovan's mystic skull ring! The boy took it eagerly and found it absolutely undamaged. Operator 5 laughed as he wiped the ring clean on a handkerchief and returned it to the deeply relieved boy.

"Gee, Jimmy! I don't see how you did it! I saw you hammer the ring flat and put it into the gun. There wasn't anything tricky about the egg I brought from the refrigerator, either. My ring was inside that egg, all right—but I don't see how it got there!"

"It's really very simple, Tim," Jimmy Christopher answered. "I didn't actually hammer your ring, at all. Look at this!"

He took up the pistol and removed from it the wad of paper. From the bore fell a bit of smashed metal—a ring resembling Tim's, but made of soft lead. Operator 5 continued briskly: "Now here's the whole secret.

"When I borrowed your ring from you, I had this other one

concealed in my hand. I switched it for your ring, keeping yours out of sight in my palm, while I hammered the other one flat I dropped the fake ring into the gun, and then took the egg from you.

"The egg was absolutely unprepared, of course. But, unseen by you, I dropped your ring into the egg-cup just before I put the egg in. The ring then lay under the egg in the cup and when I forced the egg down a little, the pressure was enough to break the shell at the lower end where the ring lay. I then poked into the egg from above with the hook and appeared to remove your ring from the inside of it. What I really did was to reach completely through the egg with the hook, catch hold of your ring—and there it was!"

"You sure had me worried!" Tim exclaimed.

Operator 5 smiled, returned the apparatus to his workshop. When he came back, his face was solemn. "No word yet from Z-7! I can't wait any longer!"

HE STRODE to the telephone and called the number of Secret Intelligence Headquarters M-9. He exchanged signals quickly and Z-7's voice sounded over the line. Operator 5 asked anxiously:

"Chief—have you been able to reach our men in Calkar?"

Z-7 answered ringingly. "No! We have been cut off completely from all direct avenues of communication. I have tried to relay messages through London and Paris and Rome—without result."

"We must open new lines at the earliest possible moment,

then, Chief!" Operator 5 declared. "I intend to attempt to do that myself."

"You?" Z-7 blurted. "But it means going to Balkaria! It means acting as a spy in a foreign, hostile country!"

"I know that, Chief—but it must be done!"

"It's a terrific risk!" Z-7 protested. "You must realize the danger. If you are caught acting as a spy in Balkaria, I will be able to do nothing to help you. Spies, once they are captured by the enemy, must be repudiated by their own governments. And the penalty for espionage in wartime is the firing-squad!"

"The task of opening new lines of communication through Balkaria, Chief," Jimmy Christopher answered firmly, "is of the utmost importance. It must be done! Unless it is done, we are doomed. But that is only one reason for my going to Balkaria. If possible, the real situation behind the threatened Mexican uprising must be found. It is a job I must tackle myself, Chief. There is no time to be lost.

"Please provide me with a passport, an identity card and other necessary papers. I will want photographs and minute descriptions of our agents in Balkaria—all available information. I must be provided with a Balkarian military uniform. Make the preparations, Chief, for I will be ready very soon!"

"I will do so at once!"

"I am coming to M-9 at once, Chief. It will be necessary for us to make a fast trip to Washington before I leave the United States. Please order a plane made ready—I'll join you immediately!"

Operator 5 turned grimly from the telephone to find Tim

119

Donovan and Diane Elliot gazing at him anxiously. Hurriedly he got into his coat. He said quietly: "You're coming with me, Tim!" And the boy bounded into the hall. He returned pulling on a broken-billed cap as Diane Elliot came to Operator 5 anxiously.

"I know nothing can stop you now," the girl declared tightly. "Oh, Jimmy, I—I'll be thinking of you constantly. Be careful, Jimmy—for me!"

Impulsively she tightened her arms around him; and Jimmy Christopher gazed into her shining, anxious eyes. His lips felt the warmth of hers, and he turned away quickly.

"Jimmy!" she exclaimed as he opened the door. "I know you've got to do it. The whole world's at war—but I want you to come back! You've got to come back, Jimmy Christopher!"

A smile tightened Operator 5's lips as he strode through the door. Tim Donovan hurried down the steps at his side. Diane Elliot stood motionless, listening as the entrance opened and clicked shut. Her small hands formed into fists and tears brought a glimmering light into her eyes.

ACROSS A desk on which lay documents of international importance, Operator 5 faced the President of the United States.

The Chief Executive of the nation, grave-faced, stood in a dim glow of light. Z-7 and Tim Donovan were at Operator 5's shoulder. They were alone in the President's study.

Z-7 had informed the President of Operator 5's contemplated action. Upon their arrival at Washington by plane, Jimmy Christopher had found waiting for him a summons to the White

House. With the Washington Chief and Tim, he had responded at once. The President had greeted him with a warm handclasp.

"Operator 5," the Chief Executive asked quietly, "your preparations are made?"

"I am ready, Mr. President!"

The President said levelly, "You are acting with characteristic courage, Operator 5. But I must express my admiration and my fervent hope that you will succeed. Hour by hour the Mexican situation becomes more threatening. It is doubly dangerous because we do not know at what hour the revolutionists will strike, or in what manner they intend to throw their force against us. If their action is sufficient to cut us off from control of the Panamá Canal, it will be a staggering blow." *

"I realize that fully, Mr. President," Jimmy Christopher answered promptly.

"What are your plans?" the President asked.

"I will proceed to Calkar by the quickest route," Operator 5 answered. "I intend to attempt to cross the Balkarian border through Switzerland."

"Even though Switzerland is neutral," the President replied,

---

* AUTHOR'S NOTE: It is a little known fact that in Columbia and the Republic of Panamá there are, living as farmers, enough Japanese reservists to equal the normal garrison of the Canal Zone. Though the American defenses possess the advantage of modern fortifications, hidden batteries and heavy armament, a skillfully directed sabotage attack could succeed in obstructing the Panamá Canal, thus cutting off vital naval traffic. The President is speaking with this knowledge in mind.

"you will face grave danger there. It is swarming with espionage and counterespionage agents. The Swiss government is in a dangerous situation and is alert to protect itself from possible embroilment in the war in every possible way. Your mission may be discovered even before you reach the Balkarian border unless you exercise every precaution."*

"I am aware of the spy danger I must pass through before I ever come near the Balkarian border, Mr. President," Operator 5 answered.

"Once you are across that border," the President continued, "you will face an even greater peril—especially since there is no way of communicating with us, and because you will have great difficulty in contacting our agents there. By the way, are you going alone?"

"Tim Donovan is coming with me, Mr. President," Operator 5 answered. "He realizes the danger. He may be able to get results where one of our regular operators would fail."

The President gazed with frank admiration at the tough Irish lad. He extended his hand, and Tim Donovan gripped it. The President's eyes turned to Operator 5.

---

* AUTHOR'S NOTE: Switzerland is the only one of the European neutrals which is completely surrounded by nations engaging in the second World War. Because of this dangerous situation, she has become a large manufacturer of arms. War Minister Rudolph Minger recently declared: "It has come to my knowledge that a German plan exists for the invasion of Switzerland.... It is high time for Switzerland to act." He asked for a military budget of 120,000,000 Swiss francs instead of the usual 92,600,000.

"Goodbye! God be with you!" Over the historic desk, the hand of the Chief Executive gripped the hand of Operator 5.

CHAPTER 9
HIDDEN EYES WATCH

IN THE humming inner office of Secret Intelligence headquarters WDC-13 in Washington, Z-7 paced the floor nervously. His fingers tendoned together behind his back; his black eyes smouldered. He whirled each time a dispatcher brought a new report from the communications room and read it eagerly; each time his shoulders sagged with despair.

An empty period had followed the last message received from Jimmy Christopher—a code radiogram sent from aboard the ship carrying him to Europe. Days had passed without word from him. Each hour had added to Z-7's anxiety. He had directed the operations of the United States Intelligence Service in all parts of the globe feverishly while he waited.

A dictaphone on the desk buzzed. He tipped a cam and a metallic voice issued from it: "We have Carlo Hapag here, Chief!"

"Bring him in!"

He straightened as a dispatcher hurried from the communications room.

"Word has come from Operator 5 by cable—in code!"

Z-7 snatched the message. He peered at cabalistic words—a communication couched in one of the most intricate ciphers

A deafening crash sounded as the heavy bumper struck the iron gate.

in use by the system. "Take it to the cipher room. I want that translation as soon as possible!"

The dispatcher hurried away with the message as a knock sounded. At Z-7's command, the door opened. Three men strode into the room. Two—United States Intelligence operators—

Two hinged sections flew open with jarring force!

were holding the arms of the third; the man between them was masked by a black handkerchief tightened over his eyes. At Z-7's word, the blind was snatched away, disclosing the prisoner's swarthy face, eyes blinking in the glare.

"Carlo Hapag," the Washington Chief declared grimly, "we

know you are a secret agent of the Balkarian government. You succeeded in tapping one of our special teletype lines, and you intercepted certain important secret dispatches. The evidence we hold against you is enough to bring the death penalty upon you with no delay. What have you to say?"

The eyes of the spy blazed defiantly. "You do not frighten me with your promise of death. I am ready to accept the penalty— gladly, because your country will pay for my death with the death of your most valuable agent. I have informed the Balkarian secret police that Operator 5 is attempting to reach Calkar!"

"What?" Z-7 strode forward threateningly, his fists clenched, his black eyes glinting. "What did you say?"

"I learned Operator 5's plans over the tapped wire!" Hapag asserted defiantly. "I immediately informed the Balkarian secret police! They are waiting for him now; they will seize him on sight! He will die before a firing squad! That is what I have to say!"

Z-7's knuckles rapped the desk. "Take this man away!" he rasped in cold fury. "Take him away before I shoot him down where he stands!"

He turned, his neck corded with tight muscles, as the two operators jerked Hapag back to the door. He strode along the corridor toward the Codes-and-Ciphers-Room. It opened as he approached, and a cryptogram expert hurried to him.

"Here's the translation of Operator 5's message!"

Z-7's eyes flashed at it:

... WDC-13... PASSING THROUGH SWITZER-

LAND… INTEND TO CROSS BALKARIAN BORDER
WITHIN THE HOUR… OPERATOR 5….

"Within the hour!" Z-7 repeated the words huskily. He strode
back to his desk glaring at the translated dispatch. He sank into
his chair numbed with a chill fear. "He has crossed the Balkarian
border by this time!"

The defiant words of Carlo Hapag echoed mockingly in his
mind as he stared into space:

"They are waiting for Operator 5 now; they will seize him on
sight! *He will die before a firing squad!*"

THE WORLD reverberated with the rumble of war. The
flames of conflict roared across Europe with ever increasing
ferocity at each passing hour. Newspapers screamed of devastating air raids upon Paris and London, of merciless gas attacks
across the Russian lines, of terrific rocket fire striking the French
fortifications along the Saar. Naval engagements brought into
use secret speed boats far more hazardous than submarines.*

From Asia flared news of military engagements in Siberia and
China, bombing raids upon Tokyo, and the reports of thousands

---

* AUTHOR'S NOTE: Revelation of the existence of these swift surface-craft
was made by military experts late in 1934. They were then known to be under
construction by Britain, France, Italy, Germany and Russia. They are capable
of sixty miles per hour and are armed with torpedoes. Showing so little above
the water and moving at such speed that no gun could hope to hit them
except by a lucky accident, so agile that not even airplanes can follow their
swift maneuvers, capable of being directed by wireless from a distance, these
boats comprise a greater menace of the sea than any submarines ever devised.

of casualties. Ever closer to the shores of the United States the flames of war reached with their threats of annihilation.

The Balkarian Front thundered with the roar of big guns spewing forth death night and day. The skies shook with the concussions of devastating battles. Patrolling airplanes swarmed, darting into enemy territory with their cargoes of death, plunging like torches before the onslaughts of anti-aircraft batteries. In the very heart of the furnace of the new World War, Balkaria flamed.

Yet, far outside the frantic city of Calkar, capital of Balkaria, dark country lay quiet. The roads had seen marching troops, but now they were empty. The skies had trembled with the drone of aircraft, but tonight they were silent. Farms, abandoned by men who had left them to fight, stretched over rolling hillsides, blanketed with a momentary peace. In all that dark territory there was scarcely a movement, hardly a light.

Along a white, hard road, through past-midnight quiet, a lone man trudged. He was wearing the uniform of a Balkarian under-officer. His heels clicked smartly, he strode—with grim purpose. He was young, clean-cut, alert; his gaze shot searchingly to each far reach of the horizon. His manner was fearless, and yet danger was his companion. He was Operator 5 of the United States Intelligence Service!

He stopped abruptly when a sound came out of the night behind him. It was the chugging of a powerful motor, a clanking of chains. A gleam of light shafted up from the far side of a hill, announcing the approach of a heavy truck. As the beams slanted downward, Operator 5 whirled to the side of the road.

He dropped flat in the shadow of a low bridge, near the opening of a dry culvert. The truck approached noisily as he lay motionless. When it clattered past, he raised to peer at it. The gigantic vehicle was mounting the slope with a heavy load, its cargo concealed under tied-down tarpaulins. In it, men wearing the uniform of the Balkarian army stood alert, rifles ready.

Operator 5 watched the truck crawl beyond the crest of the rise. He hurried after it, and again it came into sight. On the downslope, he saw it turn heavily off the road into a paved branch and cut across a hill. Again he followed it, keeping well back. The truck panted through a cut in the hill, and he shifted off the road to climb to the high point.

The great vehicle continued until it reached a heavy iron gate which barred the way. Operator 5, covered with darkness, brought a pair of night binoculars from a case slung over his shoulder and trained it upon the truck. In the shine of its headlights, other uniformed men were moving. Papers passed from hand to hand. The sentries at the gate, inspecting them, mouthed orders. The gate swung open, and the truck crawled through.

Immediately, Operator 5 saw, the way was barred again. The gate was the only opening in a high, iron-spiked fence which stretched far across the hills. Deep within the spreading space enclosed by it, in the shadows of thickly growing trees, sat a huge edifice of stone. No lights shone through its heavily curtained windows. The truck crawled along a road which encircled it, and at last passed out of sight.

OPERATOR 5 lowered his glasses; his eyes darkened thoughtfully. He turned back, hurriedly, and retraced the way he had come. When he reached the road, he began walking briskly toward Calkar. He walked until an automobile came humming behind him; it slowed, and the man at the wheel invited him to ride. While it traveled toward the capital, the Balkarian civilian spoke with hot patriotism of the advances of the Balkarian troops, of the victory they were intent upon winning. Operator 5 agreed heartily, and when the car stopped in a lighted street of the city, he expressed his thanks and left it.

He walked rapidly once more until he reached a shabby inn on an unfrequented street. Through its grimy windows, he watched men and women sitting at the tables and standing at the bar. Just inside the window, a boy in peasant clothing was slumped in a chair, apparently asleep.

Operator 5 strode into the smoke-laden atmosphere, and stood at the bar. He left his drink untouched as he glanced idly at the dozing boy. The youngster had awakened as the hand of a Balkarian officer, reeling with drink, had shaken him.

"Why do you sleep here?" the officer barked. "Why are you not at home in bed?"

The boy answered brokenly: "My father has gone to war. My mother works night and day in the factory that makes shells for my father to use. I am left alone—I am lonesome."

"Don't fear! You too will soon join the colors! We have need of every man and boy!"

The boy slumped back again. Operator 5 smiled with grim satisfaction. During the voyage across the Atlantic he had trained Tim Donovan intensively in the Balkarian tongue. The boy had maintained his disguise to perfection. Hour after hour he had loitered in this odorous bar, apparently dozing but actually sharply alert. Now, as his head settled, his gaze turned an instant to Operator 5. Then his eyes flashed at a civilian standing near Jimmy Christopher, and closed again.

Operator 5 studied that man's features intently. He stepped near. Toying with his glass, he spoke so that no one other than the man Tim Donovan had singled out could hear.

"S-6."

The man's eyes turned slowly. His manner was casual, his face unchanging, but a sudden gleam had come into his eyes. He mumbled a confused answer and began to turn away. Operator 5 spoke again.

"Forty-eight stars."

The other man peered more keenly. Operator 5 had spoken the code word by which U.S. Intelligence agents in Balkaria could recognize each other. The man demanded, in a husky whisper: "In God's name, who are you?"

"Operator 5."

"God! I thought you were one of the Balkarian secret police, trying to trick me into betraying myself! We scarcely dare take a breath. It's almost impossible to—"

"Listen carefully!" Jimmy Christopher interrupted. "You must somehow get in touch with our other agents immediately. I must see all of our agents tonight—important orders. I have taken a room upstairs under the name of Borrok."

After a moment of disarming small talk in the Balkarian tongue, S-6 moved toward the door. When he hurried away, Operator 5 sauntered across the room to the corner where Tim

Donovan was pretending to doze. He stirred the boy with a chuckle.

"Come!" he exclaimed. "I have a room upstairs. You will be able to sleep much better there than here. It is late."

"Thank you, lieutenant!" the boy exclaimed, jumping up. "You are very kind!"

OPERATOR 5 strode past crowded tables toward a stairway at the rear. His gaze searched each face. Among these apparently idle people were, probably, agents of the Balkarian secret police—an organization as ruthless and powerful as the dread GPU of Russia. Fearful stories were circulating concerning unfortunate suspects who had been seized—who thereafter had vanished from the face of the earth. Jimmy Christopher carried himself with a jaunty, confident air as Tim Donovan followed him to the stairway.

Once in the shabby room on the second floor, Operator 5 listened, to be sure that they had not been followed. "We've got to wait, Tim," he whispered. "Good work, finding S-6!"

"I recognized him from one of the photographs Z-7 gave us!" the boy whispered.

"Tim, I've a feeling that we're being watched. Keep near the door and listen!"

He turned to a large leather suitcase while the Irish lad kept on the alert. He removed clothing from it, touched a hidden catch, and lifted the leaf of a false bottom. From it he removed a small contrivance of his own devising. Unbuttoning the tunic of his uniform, he strapped it in place on his chest. He carefully replaced the tunic, and made an adjustment at his cuff.

132

"What's that?" Tim Donovan asked curiously.

"A camera, Tim. I built it so that I can take miniature photographs without anyone's being aware of it at the time. The lens is concealed in this button of my uniform. By pulling on my sleeve, I release the shutter and a new section of film automatically shifts into place. I hope to get photographs that will—"

He broke off, listening. Footfalls sounded in the hallway, came to the door, and paused. A soft knock sounded. Jimmy Christopher opened the door without hesitation. The man known as S-6 stepped inside, greeting Operator 5 in Balkarian. When the door closed his voice dropped to a whisper.

"They are coming! They will all be here soon!"

They continued to talk in Balkarian of the effects of the war on civilians as they waited. Presently they heard someone else approach the door. Operator 5 opened it and another man entered. He was short, wiry, with bright eyes and sunken cheeks—the U.S. agent designated C-8. His hand gripped Operator 5's.

"The others will join us in a few moments!"

Strained minutes passed, until a knock sounded again. The third man to enter was clad in shabby clothing; he was unshaven, weak-eyed, shambling in his step. Immediately the door closed, his manner changed electrically. He did not have a chance to speak before another knock sounded. The studious-looking man who entered—apparently a schoolteacher—seemed bewildered and uncertain until the door was locked again. The newcomers—agents F-2 and D-4—gripped Operator 5's hands with silent admiration.

Jimmy Christopher brought them close around him. They listened intently through the hum of voices from the bar until he spoke.

"We must lose no time! I have prepared a new way of communicating with WDC-13—a dangerous way—through Berlin. Your reports will be addressed to certain names at certain addresses, where they will be relayed through to Holland and then to WDC-13. Here is the list. Memorize it at once, for it must be destroyed."

OPERATOR 5 wrote rapidly on a sheet of paper. The four undercover agents studied it silently. When they nodded, he crumpled the sheet, struck a match and set it afire. It flamed to ashes in a tray, and he ground them to powder with his thumb and poured water upon it.

Again he spoke quietly: "I have traced the freight that is passing through Calkar. It is going to a tremendous stone house southeast of the city. I saw one of the shipments reach it tonight. That house is our objective."

"Yes!" S-6 exclaimed. "I learned the destination of the freight shipments, soon after our communication was cut off."

"Who lives in that house?" Operator 5 demanded.

"That, we have been unable to learn. The identity of the man who controls it is kept secret from everyone except certain high officials of the Balkarian government. He is accorded extraordinary privileges. The place is closely guarded, armed like a fortress. To approach it is to risk your life."

Operator 5 declared calmly: "We are going to penetrate that house. We must get inside it, learn who the master of it is, prove the nature of the shipments he receives." He gazed into the dismayed faces of the four agents. "I realize the danger—but we must make the attempt."

"We're with you!" S-6 declared.

"The rest of my plan I will explain later. Before we set out, there is one point which must be made absolutely clear. It is this—if any one of us should be captured, the others must make absolutely no attempt to save him. Your prime necessity is to remain free, to resume sending reports to WDC-13. Your ability to do that must not be sacrificed even for the life of a comrade."

Tim Donovan was peering into Jimmy Christopher's face intently.

"The secret police may close down on us at any time," he continued. "If we are all taken together, that will be a catastrophe. It will destroy our organization in Balkaria. Remember, above all, that your own life and your own escape are of paramount importance. I repeat, if any of you see another of us seized by the secret police, you must let that man be seized—make no attempt to help him. Those are strict orders!"

Tim blurted: "If you—"

"If I am captured, Tim," Operator 5 declared firmly, "you are to think only of making your own getaway. Keep absolutely clear of me. I expect you to follow orders."

The boy blinked as if stunned. Operator 5 moved quickly to the door and listened. He returned to say quietly: "We must wait no longer. Leave the room separately. We will meet at S-6's car outside."

S-6 gripped Operator 5's hand and left the room. One by

one the three other agents departed. Jimmy Christopher waited anxiously, then signaled Tim Donovan. They went down the stairs together and again passed through the crowded, smoky bar. Once outside, they walked rapidly in a direction opposite to that which S-6 had indicated.

They circled the block, into a narrow, bleak street. Near the corner, a sedan was parked, S-6 waiting outside it. Operator 5 glanced around quickly, and entered the car with Tim Donovan. They found the three other agents waiting. S-6 took the wheel and the car swung around the corner, rolled through the brighter light of an important street.

At the edge of the city, a chain, drawn between two kiosks, barred the way. It was a municipal customs post. From it, officers approached with a demand to see the identity cards of those in the car. They scrutinized each card minutely while Operator 5 waited in tense anxiety. The officers returned them, lowered the chain, and waved S-6 on.

The car droned out into the darkness surrounding the city. Miles away, it turned upon the road which led in the direction of the mysterious, fortified house. They were still far from it when Operator 5 ordered the car pulled off the road, across a field, and into the shadow of a clump of trees. The headlights blinked out. Jimmy Christopher stepped out into thick darkness and signaled his men to follow. He hurried back to the road with them; they crouched in a black ditch that flanked the pavement.

There they waited silently.

CHAPTER 10
THE VAULTS OF THE POWER

LIGHTS GLEAMED along the road; a snorting and chuffing sounded. The gleam and the sounds came after an interminable period of quiet. Huddled in the hollow, Operator 5 rose to see the headlamps of a truck appear at the crest of a slope. The huge vehicle rattled toward him and his men while he strove to penetrate the glare of the lights.

The truck ground past. Jimmy Christopher discerned two armed, uniformed men on the seat beside the driver; two others were near the tailgate, standing with rifles. He spoke quickly through the snarling of the motor.

"S-6, D-4! After me! Tim! Wait with the others!"

He darted onto the road, running forward. S-6 and D-4 followed him rapidly. They sprang toward the rear of the truck as one of the alert men turned. Operator 5 leaped as a rifle glittered upward. His hand grasped the barrel and tore it downward violently. S-6 and D-4 sprang at the second guard as Operator 5 cleared the tailgate. A dull crack sounded as S-6's fist felled the second of the pair. Operator 5 whispered, "Off with them!" as he sprang down. He pulled down the unconscious man who had fought him. S-6 and D-4 hurriedly lowered the other. Alertly they watched the driver's enclosed seat, ready to meet an attack—but no alarm came. They had struck swiftly and silently; and now they whirled away with the quiet movement of ghosts.

Operator 5 heeled into the ditch beside the road and lowered his man. "Take the uniform off the other one!" he commanded S-6. "Get into it! Make it fast!"

He sprang up and ran. When he reached the spot where C-8 and F-2 were hiding with Tim Donovan, he dropped down again. He issued orders quickly.

"Follow us afoot and wait—but keep clear of that house. There may be no chance for you to help. If not, return to Calkar as soon as possible. Stay near the room, Tim, and wait for me!"

"Jimmy!" the alarmed boy called as he sprang up again, but he did not pause. He sprinted back along the road as S-6 climbed up. The undercover agent had pulled the uniform off the unconscious guard and donned it. He began running with Jimmy Christopher along the road, frantically buttoning the tunic. Ahead, the huge truck was still clattering slowly on its way.

They darted behind it, gripped the tailgate, and swung over. Coming erect, they held their rifles ready, and again made sure that the men on the front seat had not taken alarm. Operator 5 warned silence; and they stood at their posts as the truck snarled on.

It soon swerved into the branch that cut through the hills. The curving road led through passes filled with darkness. When it began to snort up the last slope, the gigantic stone edifice, completely surrounded by its high iron fence, came into view. Operator 5's nerves tightened as the truck crawled toward the gate and stopped.

Again his eyes flashed warning to S-6 as uniformed sentries approached the driver. Documents passed from hand to hand and were closely examined in the light. Sentries, guns ready, marched behind the truck to peer into the faces of Operator 5 and S-6. They withstood the scrutiny with cold apprehension; the men moved on.

Iron creaked upon iron as the heavy gate swung open. Again the truck snarled on its way. Immediately it passed inside, the way was again barred; the sentries resumed their patrols. They were wearing, Jimmy Christopher noted, Balkarian uniforms; their rifles were Balkarian. The truck crawled past the high stone walls of the formidable house, then curved and came to a stop at the rear.

NEARBY STOOD a broad door of steel, set into the massive stone. The two armed men leaped from the front seat. Operator 5 and S-6 obeyed their sharp orders and assisted in untying a large sheet of tarpaulin which was stretched over the truck's freight. Beneath it were disclosed strong wooden boxes, banded with iron strips, stenciled with inscriptions.

Operator 5 noted grimly from the labels that the boxes had passed through three warring nations. Glancing up, he saw the huge iron door of the stone house swinging open. Out of it two men with rifles, wearing Balkarian uniforms, appeared. A third, in civilian clothing, strode to the rear of the truck with an imperious manner. "Down with them!" he commanded. "Lose no time!"

Under a sharp tongue-lashing, Operator 5 and S-6 were obliged to bend to the task of unloading the freight. Though the boxes were small they were astoundingly heavy; two men had to struggle to carry each of them. Jimmy Christopher and S-6, swinging one between them, carried it through the huge iron door. They brought it into a room of stone walls and stone floor, entirely bare, and deposited it.

Again and again they returned from the truck with more of the boxes while the other pair of guards alternated with them. The stacks mounted within the stone room. After an hour of backbreaking labor, the truck was emptied. Again papers passed hands, and the driver returned to his seat. His two guards followed as Operator 5 stepped close to the side of S-6.

"Stay with me!"

With the puzzled S-6 beside him, he again approached the huge door as it was closing. He stepped through alertly. Instantly the two sentries snapped their rifles down, leveled. The man who had supervised the unloading of the freight stared at Operator 5 forbiddingly. He snapped sharply. "Are you mad? Do you forget your orders? You are to return with the truck!"

"Not at all," Operator 5 answered easily. "I have brought a special dispatch from the War Office concerning this shipment. I am to deliver it and bring an answer."

"Give it to me!"

"My orders," Operator 5 insisted, unshaken, "are to deliver it to no one but—*him!*"

"He is not to be disturbed. You will have to wait!"

"Wait?" Operator 5 asked daringly. "A special message of the highest importance from the Balkarian Chief of Staff, and you say I must—"

"Even governments wait for him!…" the other man interrupted testily. "I warn you, lieutenant, if this is some trick, it's a hopeless attempt. If you have lied, you will die. It will not be the first time men have entered the walls never to leave them alive!"

Operator 5's expression did not change. "Very well," he said quietly. "We will wait."

A sharp command snapped. The ponderous door swung shut with a dull thud. Outside, the truck began to snarl as it moved toward the gate. S-6 shot a sharp glance at Operator 5's face and found him cool and poised. Again commands snapped, and a door opened to admit other men in uniform.

"Take the boxes into the vault!" To Operator 5 he snapped: "You will wait here until I take you to him."

The sharp-mannered man passed on through another heavy door. Operator 5, turning squarely toward the pile of boxes, tugged imperceptibly at his sleeve. His concealed camera functioned soundlessly; unknown to those in the stone room, a photograph was taken. Operator 5 turned again as a third door was opened, revealing a short flight of stone steps descending. A LIGHT switch snapped, and a glare fell upon an iron slab below. It was the face of a safe-door, gleaming with crisscrossing bars. Another man entered the room, faultlessly attired—a man with stiff, flaxen hair and sharp blue eyes that turned piercingly on Jimmy Christopher. Without speaking, he strode down the stone flight to the vault door. He turned a combination dial carefully, spun a wheel that withdrew the bolts. He tugged the great door open and a startling sight was revealed to Operator 5.

He peered into a vast room beyond, its walls made of stone, its space divided into compartments. In these sections, other boxes, similar to those just delivered, were stacked—scores and hundreds of them. In one section, directly ahead, shone a golden glitter—sparkling yellow metal! On stout steel shelves, ingots of virgin gold lay naked in the light, each of a size to fit into the wooden boxes.

Operator 5 stood back as the man who had opened the vault returned. Again he tugged at his sleeve, and again the hidden camera registered the scene. Immediately the uniformed men fell to work, carrying the heavy boxes into the vault, placing them in a section out of sight. Jimmy Christopher turned smartly as the stubble-headed man spoke:

"Keep your eyes up! To mention anything you may see here is to commit suicide with your lips! Follow me!"

Jimmy Christopher and S-6 stepped after the cruel-faced man into a long, narrow corridor of stone. At its end, they passed through a heavy door into a small room richly furnished. They walked on until they reached a spacious study, breathtaking in the splendor of its tapestries and appointments. At a huge carved desk, the stiff-haired man paused.

"Now, your message! You may deliver it to me here!"

"That is impossible," Operator 5 declared. "The message is in a new code. No one will be able to read it without my instructions. I am sworn to reveal the secret to no one but—*him!*"

The blue gaze sharpened again. "Very well, then," the big man declared. "You must still wait."

He turned sharply, strode from the room. The door closed tightly. S-6, about to speak, was silenced by a warning gesture from Jimmy Christopher. He circled the room quickly; then he paused. Voices, so faint that he scarcely heard them at all, reached his ears. They were issuing through a door behind the desk. He moved to it, listened, and curled his hand around the knob.

S-6 watched in alarm as Operator 5 inched the door open. Jimmy Christopher peered into a vast library, walled to the ceiling with shelves loaded with weighty tomes. The room was empty; the voices were issuing through a door at the far side of the room, partly opened, shielded by a Japanese screen of exquisite color and great age.

A low, husky voice was speaking—a voice that Operator 5 recognized instantly as that of the Masked Power!

THE WORDS were spoken slowly. "Then we are ready! You need only the signal and it is done!"

"Yes!" The second voice was sibilant. "The overthrow of the Mexican government is only a matter of hours. Our strength will crush them at once. Immediately we are in power, the way is open. The revolutionists will stop at nothing to win the rich prize you have offered them!"

The husky voice spoke again. "And the weapon you will turn against the United States is their own latest weapon of defense—the fast tank!"

"Exactly! The revolutionist forces have as many of the new tanks as they—thanks to you! In every particular, our tanks are duplicates of those of the United States. If one of ours stood side by side with one of the American units—no one would be able to tell the difference!"

"Very well." Operator 5 listened in cold amazement as the husky voice resumed. "You are to return to Mexico at once.

Assure the revolutionist leaders again that, when the United States is crushed, they will be rewarded with the territory now comprising the states of Texas, New Mexico and Arizona as well as the southern part of California. Immediately you return, order the revolution without an hour's delay."

"I will be proud!" the other said.

"At that hour we will strike the blow which will drive the United States into the new World War. The United States already knows that Balkaria is behind the revolution. The invasion will constitute an attack by a foreign power. The inevitable result is a declaration of war on the part of the United States against Balkaria, which will fling it headlong into this world conflict. Once the United States is at war, strongly attacked from the South, drawn to the side of her past European allies, threatened on the West by Japan—it is the beginning of the end!"

"The inevitable end!" the second man agreed.

"Then—" the heavy voice grew huskier, "carry your word back. The way is open to you. Lose no time. We are on the threshold of world dominion!"

Soft footfalls sounded in the screened room. Operator 5 drew back tensely; he closed the door. He turned to S-6 with his face white, his lips hard-pressed. S-6 had come to his side; every word spoken had been audible to them both. They faced each other with profound anxiety and again Operator 5's warning gesture enforced silence upon S-6.

They returned swiftly to their chairs—were scarcely seated before a door opened suddenly. The stubble-headed secretary approached, his manner guarded. "You may deliver your message now."

Operator 5 promptly stepped forward, and as promptly S-6 began to follow. A sharp command froze them: "Alone!"

Operator 5's glance warned S-6, and the agent stepped back with a shrug of simulated indifference. Jimmy Christopher stepped through the door into a thickly carpeted hallway. He was led along it to the second door beyond. There the secretary gripped his arm and brought him to a stop.

"Remember—do not dare breathe a hint of anything you may see here! We will know instantly if you disobey. The penalty is death!"

THE HUGE hand thrust open the door. Operator 5 peered into a room luxuriously furnished, lighted with a dim glow except at the broad desk sitting in the center. There a bright gleam shone from a shaded light, reflecting onto the man who stood behind it. He was a massive figure whose head was masked. Through the black fabric, his steely eyes shone. Through the doorway Operator 5 faced the Masked Power!

With brisk step, his eyes never leaving the masked head, Jimmy Christopher strode into the room. His heels clicked. He stood at stiff attention.

The man in the mask asked huskily: "You bring me a message?"

"Privately, sir."

The gray eyes shifted to the secretary standing in the doorway. Quietly, the secretary withdrew, closing the door. The masked man squared his huge shoulders and extended his hand.

"Your message!"

Operator 5's right hand moved to the pocket of his tunic. It contained no message. Inside it lay a small automatic, loaded, its catch unsnapped. Jimmy Christopher's fingers slid to its butt and gripped.

A sharp buzz sounded. The masked man behind the desk reached toward a telephone. He raised the instrument to his covered face and droned: "Yes?" He listened intently, while Jimmy Christopher stood motionless, gray eyes glittering. He snapped: "At once!" and returned the instrument to its standard. He stared, his masked head bowed, his metallic eyes shining, at Operator 5.

"You will be surprised to know," he said gutturally, "that I also have a message for you."

Sudden sounds filled the room—the quick opening of doors. Three of them flew wide at the same instant—one behind Operator 5, one on each side of him. They revealed uniformed men standing erect, rifles brought to their shoulders, eyes gleaming behind the sights—aiming full at Operator 5.

Jimmy Christopher whirled, struck cold. The hand gripping the automatic froze. He whipped back as a low laugh sounded through the black cowl. The Masked Power leaned forward intently. "My message to you? It is this: You are under arrest!"

Nine rifles leveled with deadly steadiness at Operator 5. The surging chill of danger he felt was not reflected in his darkened eyes. He smiled slowly, shrugged.

"Surely," he said in a quiet tone, "there is some mistake. I am an accredited messenger from the Balkarian War Office carrying an—"

"You are Operator 5 of the United States Intelligence Service!" the cowled man snapped.

Jimmy Christopher's heart grew cold. In the hallway beyond, he heard the heavy tramping of feet. A burst of voices sounded—a scuffle. Suddenly a shot echoed from beyond, and the noises suddenly stopped. Grimly he peered across the desk at the Masked Power as footfalls sounded again.

An officer strode into the room. The riflemen at the door behind Operator 5 stepped aside to admit others. They marched forward, with S-6 striding between them. The man's face was deathly white; his right arm was hanging loosely at his side and the stiff fingers were dripping blood. The tear of a bullet marked the sleeve above the elbow. He was brought to Operator 5's side as the Balkarian Captain stepped forward.

"Sir, we followed these men from Calkar," the officer declared to the masked man. "We had been informed by one of our agents in the United States of the identity under which Operator 5 was traveling. After he passed through the customs post tonight, we followed him here."

THE MASKED POWER peered intently at Operator 5 as two soldiers stepped forward. Their hands probed into his pockets and S-6's; they took away two guns. Grim satisfaction filled Operator 5 when the searching fingers passed unnoticingly over the flat contrivance concealed beneath his tunic—the hidden camera mechanism. They stood stiff and defiant as the Captain of the secret police declared: "The United States is not yet a participant in the war, sir. Although you are guilty of hostile espionage, of wearing the uniform of a potential enemy, nevertheless you may wish to appeal for assistance to the Ambassador from the United States."

Operator 5's mind rang with the memory of the voice of the President of the United States: "... *If you are captured by the military agents of any foreign government, we will be absolutely unable to come to your assistance. Even worse, we will be forced to deny even that you are serving the United States!*" A tight smile curved his lips as the room became silent. "I will say nothing."

"Under the circumstances, then," the Captain of the secret police declared, "we have no alternative but to impose upon you the penalty for your acts—death before a firing squad!"

The Masked Power's great hands pressed hard to the desktop. "Lose no time about it, Captain! March him out now—both of them—and kill them!"

The Captain gestured in a mild protest. "Sir, the court-martial will be only a formality, but the requirements of the Balkarian government—"

"*I* am the Balkarian government!"

The thunderous burst of wrath drove color from the face of the Captain. He snapped to attention and saluted. He stood stiff while the masked man continued with a voice ringing with rage: "I decree the death penalty upon these men to be executed without delay! You have your orders! Obey them!"

Again a swift salute. "Yes, sir!"

Operator 5 still faced the Masked Power. He gazed at the steely eyes glinting at him through the slits of the cowl. The husky voice sounded lower-toned, grating with the cruel joy of triumph.

148

"You will find an excellent location for the execution on these grounds, Captain. You will find that it is a most beautiful spot on which to die, Operator 5."

The Captain of the Balkarian secret police snapped commands. From the doorways, uniformed men advanced. They took positions smartly at the sides of Operator 5 and S-6. Another order rang; they about-faced. Heels thudding, flanked on all sides by riflemen, S-6 and Operator 5 strode out the door and into the corridor.

The man in the mask stood motionless, his glittering gray eyes peering through that door until the last of the uniformed men marched out. He heard the footfalls beat away into the quiet. He heard a door open and clank shut. From the lips hidden by the black velvet cowl, a low laugh of triumph sounded....

CHAPTER 11
FIRING-SQUAD FATE

B EYOND THE formidable iron fence which surrounded the tremendous stone edifice, darkness shrouded rolling territory. Against the blackness of a hill, within sight of it, three figures crouched. They were motionless and wordless; their anxious eyes searched the grounds. Alert, hidden by the night, having approached as close to the stone structure as they dared, C-8, F-2 and Tim Donovan waited.

They had obeyed Operator 5 and followed the truck on foot. They had seen it, after an interminable wait, snarl outward through the gate without Jimmy Christopher and S-6. Realizing that Operator 5 and S-6 had remained within the high iron barrier, they had continued to peer across the enclosed grounds, at the heavy doors. Each added moment of waiting presented new danger to them; but they did not move.

At the huge gate, uniformed men carrying rifles were on duty. Following the exit of the truck, they had fastened it with a heavy chain and a huge padlock. They marched back and forth as the three unseen watchers waited. Along the outside of the fence, other sentries patrolled, rifles on their shoulders, marching alertly from corner to corner. Guarded like a fortress, the great stone edifice lay in silence disturbed only by the beat of the sentries' heels.

At last there was an unexpected sound. The clank of a bolt sounded. The feet of marching men gritted in gravel with a steady rhythm. The three watching from the hillside strained to see, but nothing was visible in the shadows surrounding the great house. Then the strutting squad appeared in the open, led by an officer—armed men surrounding two others who were not armed!

Tim Donovan sprang up in alarm. Through the gloom, he gazed with his heart pounding coldly. "It's Jimmy!"

C-8 strained up beside the boy. "Yes! Operator 5 and S-6. They're caught!"

"God!" F-2 blurted it in horror. "It's a firing squad! They're not wasting any time!"

Tim Donovan felt his hand gripped coldly as he involuntarily started forward. C-8 grimly held him back. The secret agent declared tensely:

"Steady, kid! We can't do anything to help them now! Remember orders!"

Tim Donovan scarcely heard. He watched the uniformed squad march straight across the spacious grounds, past extensive gardens, toward a cleared grassy area near the spiked fence.

He could see Operator 5's drawn face clearly as he strode along with the soldiers. Dread widened the boy's eyes and he tugged frantically to break C-8's grasp on his hand, but the agent's fingers twined hard.

"Easy, boy! Remember what he warned us! We've got to keep at our posts! We've got to get our reports back! We can't—"

The tough little Irish lad's eyes intently followed the movements of the marching men beyond the fence. As they neared a strip of garden which flanked it, a command of the officer carried on the wind: "Halt! About face!" With the others, Operator 5 and S-6 turned. Again a command snapped, and the squad marched forward, away from the two, leaving them standing shoulder to shoulder, alone.

Tim Donovan tore his hand away from C-8's frantically. "They're going to kill him!" He started forward and C-8 darted to block his way. "Don't try to stop me! They—"

"Stay back!" C-8 whispered desperately. "There's nothing we can do! They're inside that fence and it's guarded. We're outnumbered. If we make a move, we'll all get shot down. That's why he ordered us to keep hands off! Washington expects reports—and dead men can't send them!"

From beyond the fence commands rang again. "Halt! About face!"

TIM DONOVAN stared through the gloom to see the squad whirl. They stood in a single line, facing Operator 5 and S-6 across an area of verdant grass. Near them stood the officer, sword drawn, blade glimmering....

Tim Donovan thrust C-8 aside. His hand groped at his pockets—pockets that were empty. He turned, peering into C-8's drawn face—and suddenly he leaped. He threw himself upon the secret agent and fought with the fury of a wild animal. The viciousness of the attack flung C-8 backward; he sprawled on the slope, bewildered, feeling Tim Donovan's hands tearing at his pockets. Suddenly the boy leaped up, whirled away from F-2's groping arms as the second Intelligence man rushed in.

He sprang down the slope gripping C-8's automatic. C-8 struggled up desperately. Both of them started after the fleeing boy. But Tim Donovan was running with the agility of a rabbit, eyes on the firing squad beyond the fence. They brought up short, sinking again to the ground, peering after him, winded.

Tim Donovan ran with all the strength he could summon toward the black barrier of the fence. He stumbled to a pause, his widened eyes glancing along its length. A few yards away, a sentry was marching, back turned, rifle shouldered. Tim Donovan went forward again, more slowly, taking painful precautions against making sounds. The grass stirred under his feet with a noise that alarmed him; each step seemed loud as the boom of a gun in his throbbing ears. He crept rapidly as he dared, toward the bushes of the garden that masked the lower part of the fence, and came within a few yards of the spot where Operator 5 was standing.

He saw Jimmy Christopher's head turn. Operator 5's darkened eyes peered into those of S-6. His quiet words carried to Tim Donovan: "I'm sorry, old fellow. You followed me without a question and it's brought you—"

"Hell, forget it!" S-6 answered throatily. "I've got it coming sometime and I'm ready to take it here and now."

Shoulder to shoulder, chins lifted, they faced the firing squad. The Captain's sword flashed in the dim light. His command rang: "Ready!"

Tim Donovan stared at the line of men. His chubby hand gripped hard the butt of the huge automatic. He loosened its catch and tensed to rise. Into his ears snapped the second sharp command: "Aim!"

Tim Donovan straightened. His arm lifted to level the automatic. He steadied it. He saw the sword flash again in emphasis of the coming signal—to fire.

Tim Donovan pulled the trigger!

The blasting report snatched the final command from the lips of the Captain. The bullet passed through the air near his head with waspish whine. He whirled in consternation as Operator 5 and S-6 jerked around. Tim Donovan, his whole body trembling, his finger white upon the trigger, fired again and again, swiftly.

Instantly Operator 5 sprang away as a hoarse bellow broke from the officer's lips. The rifles of the startled squad wavered. S-6 whirled as the flaming burst sounded behind him—as Tim Donovan's bullets sang through the fence at the uniformed men.

They cried out in terror and scattered. Through the dismayed chorus, the officer's scream penetrated: "Shoot them down!"

A rattling burst of fire crossed the green as Operator 5 sprang toward the shadows. S-6 leaped behind him frantically. Into thicker darkness Jimmy Christopher ducked, whirling as a second fusillade drummed. He saw S-6 wrench while running and hurtle forward to the ground. He poised to run back as S-6 rolled and raised staring eyes. "Get away! For God's sake, try to make it!"

The words sputtered through lips bubbling with blood; they ended in a cough. Operator 5 poised as S-6 dropped and went lax—lax with death. He shrank back, glimpsing a sentry running along the outside of the fence toward the spot from which the shots had come. He saw the firing squad scattering, heard the officer bellowing again: "Find him! Shoot him down!"

GRIMLY, COLD at heart, Operator 5 sped through deep shadows flanking the high iron fence. Outside it, sentries were running, their rifles flashing and ready. To attempt to get over it, Operator 5 knew, was hopeless—the very act of raising himself would make him a helpless target. He darted on, swinging past a garden plot, through the shadows of heavy trees, toward dark buildings sitting beyond the great stone house.

Behind him, men with rifles were running, scattering in a swift search. He ran on, fast as his legs could carry him, until he reached the side of the rear building. His glance along its front disclosed broad doors, closed. He sprang to one of them, latched it open, and slipped into thick darkness inside. He caught the smell of gasoline and oil and in the gloom discerned the outlines of heavy cars in their stalls.

He slipped to the side of one of them, peered at the dash to find the ignition locked. Hastily he turned to the hood and raised it. His fingers sought wires and found them. Rapidly tracing them, he gripped one and bent its screwed-down lug rapidly back and forth until the metal snapped off. He shifted it to another terminal and thrust it hard beneath another lug. Swiftly, then, he moved to the garage doors, unbolted them, eased them outward an inch.

He darted to the wheel of the heavy sedan. He opened the choke and thrust at the starter. A snarl answered, a burst of quiet power. He glanced around swiftly to make sure that all windows were closed, and he pulled the shift-lever back. He tensed, listening—and suddenly he released the clutch.

The weighty car spurted forward. Its front bumper cracked against the doors and they flew open. Operator 5 sent the car whirring from the garage and switched to high gear. Swiftly he shot it to the road that curved behind the stone structure. As he wheeled it past the corner, he saw the dark forms of soldiers running toward him, heard the spiteful reports of rifles, and heard violent impacts shake the car.

The glass pane at Operator 5's right became starred with white where the bullets hit. The glass withstood the power of the slugs. Jimmy Christopher grimly realized that the car was armored, that the panes were impenetrable, that he was riding in protection devised for the Masked Power! Again and again bullets spanged against the body and frosted the windows as he sent the car roaring past the house, swerving down the road which led to the iron gate.

At the barrier, sentries were gathered, rifles raised. Fire spat from the weapons and the bullets smashed hard against the windshield. Through the misted glass, Operator 5 saw that the gate was closed behind them, fastened by the chain and padlock. He tightened at the wheel, bracing himself. He drove the tremendous car straight at the gate. He ducked low, lips drawn tight across his bared teeth, and plunged the car ahead under full power.

A deafening crash sounded as the heavy bumper struck the ironwork. Under the terrific momentum of the car, the bar of the gate bent and snapped from its socket. The chain clicked tight and disintegrated into burst links. The two hinged sections flew open with a force that jarred the heavy stone posts on their foundations. The sedan swerved dangerously to the side of the road as Operator 5 jerked up.

He twisted it back as rifle bullets clanged to the rear of the body. Pressing the accelerator hard, he swerved around a bend in the road that led through the cut in the hill. He twisted aside to peer through the cracked glass—and suddenly his foot shot to the brake. In the darkness of the pass, he glimpsed a movement, a running figure. Sight of it shot a hot surge through Operator 5 and a name burst from his lips: "Tim!"

Smoking brakes slowed the car in the deep gloom of the cut. Operator 5 reached to uncatch the far door. He saw the boy leap aside and he called again, "Tim! In! Quick!" An inarticulate cry answered. Tim Donovan sprang from the wall of the cut. He gripped the door as Operator 5 again pressed the accelerator; he scrambled inside as the sedan shot ahead with a roar.

"Jimmy!" the boy exclaimed chokingly. "Are you all right, Jimmy?"

"Never touched me, Tim!" Operator 5 blurted. "You certainly got me out of a tight place!"

"I couldn't let 'em do that to you!"

Operator 5 twisted the car to send it upon the main highway. He pressed the accelerator hard to the floorboards and switched on the lights. The shafts showed him a clear way, a road stretching far through open country. His hands went white as he gripped the wheel.

"We can't use this car long! We've got to get across the border between roads somehow." The roaring power of the great car sent it like wheeled lightning through the night....

IN THE inner office of secret Intelligence Headquarters WDC-13 in Washington, Z-7 sat tensely at his desk. From the adjoining communications room came the continual bustle of tense activity. Over secret wires and through the ether, dispatches were flooding to this point of focus. At a report which had reached WDC-13 long hours ago, the Washington Chief peered haggardly.

It had come by cable, relayed in code through Berlin and Holland, and it read tersely:

... WDC-13... OPERATOR 5 CAPTURED... HIS WHEREABOUTS AND TIM DONOVAN'S UNKNOWN... C-8 CB....

Since that startling message there had been only silence—blank uncertainty concerning the fate of Operator 5 and Tim Donovan.

Z-7 realized, as few other men could, the hopeless turmoil prevailing in the war-torn countries of Europe. Out of the conflict came dispatches that could only sketch the most important developments of the new World War. Unmentioned in these chaotic hours, unknown to the world at large, battles were being fought, cities had been attacked by air, new bombardments were occurring. Unnoticed in the toll of destruction, unknown even to the homes from which they had come, the death-lists of thousands of combatants mounted. Of the discovery and execution of spies, scarcely any word reached even their headquarters. Of this unseen army, Operator 5 was one—obscured by the smoke of raging war.

Out of the communications room, a wide-eyed dispatcher hurried with a sheet pasted with teletype strips. He thrust it at Z-7 and exclaimed: "A message from Lucerne, in Code 7. It might be from Operator 5!" Z-7 snatched it in trembling fingers and whirled to the door. He strode into the Codes- and Ciphers-room, where men were working intently under bright lights at littered desks.

"Translate it! Get at it fast!"

A spectacled expert drew a code book close. His eyes flashed from page to page as his pencil scratched on a pad. Z-7, bending anxiously over his shoulder, read the words as they formed:

... SUCCEEDED CROSSING BALKARIAN BORDER

NOW SAFE BOTH RETURNING AT ONCE....

Z-7 breathed in profound relief. "Thank God! He's coming back!"

For beneath the terse translation, the pencil of the cipher expert traced the coded signature of Operator 5!

CHAPTER 12
PRELUDE TO DOOM

FROM THOUSANDS of roaring presses, newspapers streamed, their front pages blotted with news that struck terror across the United States:

Revolution Crushes Mexican Rule!
Officials Assassinated, Army in Command!
Balkarians Lead Bloody Uprising!

Over coast-to-coast radio networks, the voices of news commentators brought to startled millions the latest developments in the flood of war that had carried to the borders of the United States:

"Striking suddenly and powerfully, organized revolutionists acted this afternoon to overthrow the Mexican government. All of Mexico broke into turmoil as the uprising spread like wildfire. Few reliable news dispatches have come out of the chaotic situation, and details are lacking, but it is known that the revolution presents an unparalleled danger to the security of the United States.

"The highest officials of the Mexican government are reported assassinated by the revolutionist leaders. Loyal commanders of the Mexican army have also been slain by the revolters. The army has passed under the control of the revolutionists, and some of the ringleaders are known to be Balkarian officers and agents. The situation is fraught with serious implications for the United States. Any hostile move by the revolutionists will certainly result in forcing the United States into armed conflict.

"Realizing this, the people of the United States have rushed protests to Washington against our entrance into the European conflict. Business is almost at a standstill under the spell of terror that is sweeping from coast to coast. Those opposed to war, as well as those advocating it, are inciting riots in many American cities.

"The President is striving to keep a rebellious Congress in hand. Meeting even now, it is feared that Congress will vote a declaration of war, immediately any hostile move is directed against us from Mexican territory. All eyes are turned toward the south as Washington waits. Hour by hour, the situation is developing into the gravest this nation has ever faced!"

The thunder of war had begun to echo, growing ever louder. The forces of the United States government were being marshaled to meet the crisis. Diplomats hurried to and from the White House, maintaining strict silence to the press. Governmental wires hummed with dispatches relating each new development. Unknown to the people of the United States, the organization of the Intelligence Service functioned at its utmost pitch of efficiency.

The activity of the Service centered now in a quiet brownstone house just west of Central Park, in New York City. To all appearances it was merely another of a score of identical homes along that quiet street; but within its walls Intelligence Headquarters M-9 was located. A month ago the dwelling was empty; a month hence it might be deserted; but now it hummed with a steadily mounting nervous tension.

In an inner office, surrounded by files containing data which was duplicated in every other Intelligence headquarters in the country, Z-7 worked at fever pitch. As he read dispatches and issued orders, his glance shot again and again to an electric clock on his desk. Dark anxiety shone in his eyes as the red second hand spun away the minutes. In the light his face shone haggard while he waited.

The sound of a buzzer jerked him toward a dictaphone. Out of it, a voice rasped—a voice that sent a surge of profound relief through the Washington Chief. It declared succinctly: "Operator 5 is here!"

"Bring him in at once!"

Z-7 sprang up as the door of the inner office opened. Through it strode Jimmy Christopher. Tim Donovan kept at his side as he approached the desk. Z-7 gripped Operator 5's hand hotly, his eyes shining with admiration.

"Thank God, you're back, and safe! I have given copies of your reports from shipboard to the President and the Secretary of War, and they are being acted upon."

OPERATOR 5 smiled slowly. "Tim Donovan made it possible for me to get back. We succeeded in getting across the Balkarian border together; we were forced to swim Lake

161

Winstaf to reach Switzerland—the rest presented no problem. Now, Chief—!"

A dispatcher hurried into the room. "Teletype message in double code from Mexico, Chief!"

"Get it translated at once! I've been waiting for that!" Z-7 turned to face Operator 5 again, as the dispatcher hurried down the hallway. "Thank God you have forewarned us! The President has decided upon a gesture by which he hopes to discourage an invasion across our southern border."

"In what way, Chief?" Jimmy Christopher asked quickly.

"By revealing the extent of our defenses against such a move," Z-7 explained. "We have just released to the press full details concerning our fast tank corps. We are allowing the people to learn that we have thousands of these tanks ready. We have determined to make a gigantic display of them publicly. The President is leaving Washington even now to review the tank units at Laredo, Texas."

"Laredo!" Jimmy Christopher blurted. "That's directly on the Mexican border! It is a point at which the revolutionist attack is sure to center when they strike!"

"Exactly—that is why it was chosen," Z-7 declared. "It is a dangerous move—the President realizes that. Yet he is determined to make it. The first reason is to reassure the people of the United States by displaying our defensive tank strength. The second is to warn the revolutionists against any move upon us. We hope that this gigantic demonstration will stifle the threatened invasion from Mexico before it begins."

"But if it fails to stop that invasion, Chief," Operator 5 declared, "the President will be in the zone of greatest danger!"

"He realizes that, also, but he is determined to go through with the plan. The announcement of it is being made now. Once it is made, we dare not change our plans. The President cannot fail to appear at Laredo and review the tank units there. To do so would seem to be a confession of fear. It would send an even worse wave of terror rushing across the United States. It would actually encourage the invasion. It must be done!"

Operator 5's eyes darkened. "Good Lord, Chief, don't you realize the Balkarian agents are confident of the success of the invasion? Since their tanks are duplicates of ours, they must already know our strength. They will make their invasion regardless! The President's gesture will not stop them!"

Z-7 grew pale. "We will take every possible means of protecting the President. If he should be killed during this crisis, the result will be chaos—the end of the United States! But we are helpless now to do anything but go ahead with the plan."

"When," Operator 5 demanded anxiously, "is the President to review the tank units?"

"Tomorrow morning."

"Tomorrow morning!" Operator 5 blurted. "Chief, the invasion is scheduled to take place at noon tomorrow. It is Friday, the thirteenth, as I warned you! The President will actually be on the border when the attack comes!"

"I know! I know! But it is too late now!"

Jimmy Christopher straightened. "Very well, Chief. We must make the best of it. I think the warning gesture will fail, but let us hope it will not. In the meantime, we must lose no time about preparing our evidence to present to the world powers. Here, Chief, is photographic evidence to back up the reports I have sent you!"

Operator 5 placed on the desk before Z-7 a small cartridge of film no larger than a revolver bullet. "I have not had the means of developing them, Chief. The negatives must be prepared at once and enlargements made. They are photographs of the gold vaults of the Masked Power. Into those vaults, Chief, has gone already a good part of the world's supply of gold."

Z-7 closed the tiny roll of film in his hand. "We will go ahead at once, first approaching the Ambassadors of the warring countries. Pray God they will listen, and realize the appalling plan that has plunged them into war. They must be made to see that they cannot hope to save themselves from destruction except by ending the war and making it impossible for any munitions combine to control them again."

FROM THE Codes- and Ciphers-room the dispatcher hurriedly returned. He handed to Z-7 the translated message from Mexico. Operator 5 stepped close to read the startling words:

... M-9 BY WDC-13... OUR AGENTS IN VALIENTE DECLARE THOUSANDS OF TANKS HELD IN READINESS... EXACT DUPLICATES OF U.S. TANKS... OUR DEFENSES EQUALLED OR EXCEEDED BY EQUIPMENT OF REVOLUTIONISTS FORCES... COMMANDERS PREPARED TO STRIKE SOON...

MCM....

"Good God!" Z-7 exclaimed. "I ordered those men to find verification of your reports, Operator 5, and they certainly have! Tanks that are duplicates of ours—as many, perhaps more, than we have! If those two fleets of tanks face each other it will develop into one of the most terrific battles in the history of the world!"

"Confusion, Chief!" Jimmy Christopher exclaimed. "That is the weapon they are aiming to use to strengthen their tank invasion. Tanks exactly like ours attacking! In the battle, Chief, those ranks will mingle. The result will be that our tank crews will be unable to tell friend from foe. They will fear to fire upon any tank for fear of destroying their own strength. The invaders will drive ahead because they know their objective—and the element of uncertainty will hold us almost powerless to stop them!"

Z-7's fists clenched. "We must take steps to remove their advantage. I will urge the War Department to order all Tank Corps commanders to instruct that new insignia be painted on our tanks at once. In that way we may hope—"

"I'm afraid, Chief," Operator 5 declared, "that a measure as simple as that is doomed to failure. There are Balkarian spies in our tank corps—otherwise the nature of our tanks could never have leaked through to Mexico. They will inform the invaders immediately how our tanks are marked and the result will be that the invading tanks will carry the same markings. Even after the invasion starts, it will be possible for the hostile tanks to carry markings duplicating ours. "No, Chief! We most find some other way of differentiating our tanks from those of the enemy—a way that they cannot detect."

"How can we do that?" Z-7 demanded.

Operator 5 answered promptly. "I have a plan, Chief. It cannot be put into execution until the invasion actually begins, and it may not succeed, but it is the only gamble we can take. Those enemy tanks will be obliged to cross the Rio Grande before they strike United States territory. What is the condition of that river—?"

"I have reports that the Rio Grande is practically dry," Z-7 answered. "The invading tanks will be able to cross it without difficulty."

"But there they will be obliged to move slowly," Jimmy Christopher declared. "Very well, Chief. When they reach the river they will have to mass along its length. That will present our opportunity. Order a special plane prepared—a plane equipped with a liquid sprayer connected with its exhaust. The Army has experimented with several of these spray units and used them for fighting insect pests on farmlands. One of them must be made ready and held for my use as soon as possible."

"Yes, but what—?"

"Send to the commanding officer at Laredo this formula," Operator 5 continued crisply, sitting at the desk. "Instruct him to have sufficient of it made up to completely fill the spray-unit five times." He wrote rapidly on a pad. "Instruct him that the mixture is not dangerous, but that a heat reaction will take place. Put it on the wires immediately, Chief!"

Z-7 PUZZLED, strode with the scribbled sheet into the

communications room. Leaving it with a dispatcher, he returned to find Operator 5 rising thoughtfully with another written page in his hand.

"What is that stuff, Operator 5?"

"Merely a mixture which continues to generate heat within itself for a long period, because of a slow chemical reaction," Operator 5 answered. "In other words, the mixture emanates infrared rays.*

"I intend to make use of them somehow for differentiating our tanks from those of the enemy," Operator 5 declared. "Here, Chief, is another order to be transmitted to the War Department at once. It is necessary that special goggles be prepared for all members of the tank crews, and for all airplane pilots and observers who will participate in an attempt to repulse the invasion. It will require fast work to make these goggles and to distribute them, Chief, so no time must be lost!"

"What are they?"

"Goggles provided with lenses stained with Dicyanin A.**

---

* AUTHOR'S NOTE: As Operator 5 here declares, infra-red rays are not of an obscure or mysterious character. They are wave radiations ranging through nine octaves, from 8,000 to $4x10^6$, and lie in the band directly beneath light-waves visible to the human eye. Infra-red rays, being simply heat waves, are radiated from many sources—the sun, the stars, steam radiators, electric toasters, and warm-blooded animal bodies, for instance.

** AUTHOR'S NOTE: Dicyanin A is a synthetic dye of the quinoline class. It enables the human eye to see farther along the spectrum than usual, and so brings into visibility the infra-red rays. Commercially it is used for sensi-

They are absolutely necessary. Combined with the infrared mixture, they will—"

The telephone jangled, and at the moment a dispatcher looked into the office: "Telephone call for Operator 5!"

Jimmy Christopher took up the instrument quickly. The voice that came over the line was that of Diane Elliot.

"Jimmy!" she exclaimed. "It's so good to hear your voice again! I've waited ages since Z-7 told Dad you were safe and coming back."

Operator 5 broke in earnestly. "Lord! It's great to hear your voice, too, Di.

Have you and Dad been watching—?"

"We've been keeping Shepard Hunt in sight, Jimmy," the girl answered quickly. "It's been a real job, but we've done it. He's haunted the pier every time a ship from Europe docked, looking for someone. I was watching him several days ago when he seemed to spot a man. He attempted to follow, but something went wrong—he was shaken off. He immediately shifted to a second man and trailed him.

"Dad and I took turns following him then, while he continued to keep this second man in sight. The trail went down to the waterfront again when the *Ultima* docked this morning. The second man met a third there, and they went together to the Monopole Hotel on Park Avenue. Hunt followed the two of

---

tizing photographic plates to these rays, and with these plates photographs may, be taken of warm bodies in complete darkness.

them, as I followed Hunt. He watched the hotel, and I watched him.

"He seemed to be doing his best to identify and locate the two men in the hotel, and I think he succeeded. Only a short time ago he went upstairs, apparently having found out where their rooms are. I took a chance and followed. He knocked at Room 1521, and there was no answer. He went down again and succeeded in renting Room 1621 for himself—the room directly above. He's there now, Jimmy. I'm telephoning from the lobby."

"Good girl! It means that Hunt is getting close to results. Wait where you are, Di, and telephone Dad to bring the roadster around to the Monopole. I'm leaving for there immediately. In the meantime, watch sharp!"

He turned from the telephone, to Z-7. "Chief, an important lead! Di has given me a report that means the Masked Power has apparently returned to the United States. My only hope of finding him is the lead Diane has given me."

He paused, peering at Tim Donovan. "Old-timer, you're coming with me. In case it's impossible for me to get back by the time the invasion takes place, Chief, Tim will bring full information to you.

"Remember, Chief, urge all haste on the War Department on the preparation and distribution of the goggles. Make sure the plane is ready at Laredo as soon as possible. And wait for word from me!"

He hurried out the door of the inner office with Tim Donovan at his side.

CHAPTER 13
THE MASK OF DEATH

UNDER THE blazing marquee of the Monopole Hotel on Park Avenue, Operator 5 and the Irish lad left a taxi. Newsboys on the corners were screaming the latest editions, shouting of renewed riots in the United States, of the extraordinary session of Congress in which sentiment was rising toward a declaration of war should the Balkarian revolutionists move toward the Mexican border. Jimmy Christopher's face was grave as he strode into the sumptuous hotel lobby.

"The worst of it is, Tim," he said quietly, "that we are powerless to act unless the invasion actually begins. We dare not make an aggressive move. We would seem the instigator in the eyes of the world. We can do nothing but wait for the invasion to strike at us across the border—and when it comes, hope to be able to repulse it. Whether or not we can succeed in stopping that invasion is the greatest gamble we ever faced."

Tim Donovan's eyes shone anxiously. As they neared the elevators, Jimmy Christopher glimpsed Diane Elliot sitting in one of the huge chairs. His eyes flashed a warning to her; she gave no sign of recognition. He strode to a writing desk near her, took up a sheet of paper, and began to scribble.

"Can you hear me, Di?" he asked.

"Yes!"

"Stay right where you are. Keep watching for either of the two men whom Hunt followed. If they happen to come in, ring his room at once. Unless I answer, don't speak. Is Hunt still up there?"

"Yes!"

Operator 5 crunched the sheet of paper, tossed it into the wastebasket, and rose. With Tim, he strode to the elevators. At the sixteenth floor they alighted. Operator 5 led the way through a quiet corridor and paused at the door numbered 1621—the room Shepard Hunt had rented. He knocked and waited; no answer came.

He knocked again and still there was no answer. Warning Tim to keep on watch, he drew his pack of master-keys from his pocket. He worked quickly and deftly; the bolt withdrew. He stepped quickly into the hotel room with Tim following, and closed the door.

It was empty. The bed was ruffled; an ashtray was filled with cigarette stubs, and on the desk lay the room key. Operator 5 glanced about quickly, then stepped to the window. The city lights gleamed below; the East River was a black strip beyond which Brooklyn sparkled. One of the casements was open; air was gusting in. An expression of surprise passed Operator 5's lips, and he leaned forward.

Tied to the center bar of the casement windows was a sheet; it was wound into a rope that dangled to the window below. A dim light was shining through the panes of room 1521. Jimmy Christopher listened, heard no sound, and risked a call: "Hunt!... Hunt!"

There was no response. Operator 5 straightened as the telephone jangled. He strode to it. He answered: "Yes?"

Diane Elliot's voice exclaimed: "Jimmy! One of the men in 1521 has just gone up in the elevator. He's the second—the one that came on the *Ultima* this morning!"

"Thanks, Di! Keep watching!"

Operator 5 turned to the window quickly again. He realized that Shepard Hunt had seized an opportunity to search the room below: Hunt must be inside it now. The return of his quarry was a threat. Jimmy Christopher strode to the window, curled his hands around the roped sheet, and poised on the sill.

"Jimmy—what're you going to do?" Tim Donovan asked. "Look out!"

Operator 5 peered down into sheer space. Sixteen stories below lay the pavement of a side street. A fall would mean certain death. Grimly Operator 5 swung over the sill and hung, gripping the sheet.

"Stay here, Tim! Keep—"

A sudden burst of voices sounded below him—voices issuing from the open window of room 1521. A crash sounded, as of a chair overturning. Flatly, the report of a gun blasted out into the night. Operator 5's hands whitened as he dangled. Then he lowered himself.

Tim Donovan peered down at him in wide-eyed concern. Operator 5 slipped toward the lower end of the sheet, aware that it must be visible through the window, that he was exposing himself to a dangerous disadvantage. He swung in the light shafting out of the room and peered at a scene which froze him. AGAINST THE side wall of the room, Shepard Hunt was slumped, his face pasty, his hands clutching at his chest. Through

172

the fingers of that hand, red seeped. In the air hung a haze of powder-smoke and through it, a second man was peering at Hunt. He was dark-faced, evil-eyed; he was crouched forward with automatic leveled, his lips drawn from gleaming teeth.

Operator 5 twisted himself sharply, gripped the edge of the window. The sound of his heels on the sill twisted the dark-faced man about. The automatic gleamed an arc in the light as Jimmy Christopher leaped. He flung himself full upon the swarthy man, his hand snapping to the wrist that held the automatic even as it barked.

The bullet flaked plaster from the wall as Operator 5 flung the man with the gun backward. They sprawled to the carpet, struggling savagely. Jimmy Christopher found himself battling a man of appalling strength, swift in his movements as a wild animal. He whipped the gun away as he drew to his knees. He struck a swift, sharp blow of stiff fingertips to the temples of the dark-faced man—and rose.

The automatic spilled from the lax fingers. The dusky face went blank. Operator 5 bent, listened to the faint beating of the fallen man's heart and smiled with cold satisfaction. His blow had paralyzed a nerve center which would render his assailant unconscious for almost an hour.

"Jimmy!" Operator 5 turned to see Tim Donovan dangling on the roped sheet outside the window. The frantic boy clambered in hastily. Operator 5 spoke a reassuring word, turned quickly to Shepard Hunt, who was still leaning against the wall, hands clutched to his chest, eyes glazing.

"He's—he's—"

Jimmy Christopher gripped Shepard Hunt's arms. Hunt sagged forward strengthlessly, a fluttering gasp tearing from his throat. Operator 5 lifted him gently, carried him to the bed. He bent above the bleeding wound and carefully inspected it. His head wagged hopelessly as he straightened, and found Hunt staring again, breathing in torture.

"Steady!" Operator 5 warned. "You've got to have a doctor. That bullet—"

"It's no use!" Hunt blurted. "He got me—I know I'm going! For God's sake—listen!"

Jimmy Christopher bent close to hear the whispered words. "That man, Hunt!" he exclaimed. "Who is he?"

"Don't know—real name," Hunt exclaimed huskily. "Connected with—masked man—know that. Listen! Saw Masked Power—two days ago! He's here—this country! I— tried to follow—lost him. God, I—"

"Easy!"

Hunt spoke with breathless rapidity. "I followed him—got off boat. Passed letter to man—waiting for him. I lost—Masked Power in crowd!—followed other one.

"Man who took letter—lieutenant of Masked Power. This morning he—met *Ultima*—man on the floor came on it. I don't know—what's up, but—he's with Masked Power. That's—all I can help. Thought I'd find something here, but—God, I—!"

"Careful—don't talk anymore!" Operator 5 cautioned. "Save your strength!"

Shepard Hunt moaned and his eyes closed. Jimmy Christopher felt his feeble pulse and knew that the man had not long

174

to live. He turned away quickly, bent over the dark-skinned foreigner. He brought papers from the unknown man's pockets, and inspected them.

He found a passport issued to Raffaele Carrucci, and folded into it was a telegram. Its notations showed that it had been sent in the city only a few hours ago, that Carrucci must have received it just before entering the room to find Hunt searching it. Its message was brief:

ARRANGEMENTS MADE STOP SEE HIM TONIGHT STOP MUST TAKE YOU TO HIM STOP WAIT

CUPO

Operator 5 pondered the message intently. He thrust it into his pocket, turned quickly to Tim Donovan: "Old-timer, Dad should be downstairs now with the roadster. You know the compartment beneath the seat. Take the case from it and bring it right up. Warn Diane to keep on watching, and to ring this room if the other of the two men shows up."

Operator 5 let the boy into the hallway; he hurried to the elevators. Once Tim Donavan was gone, Jimmy Christopher stepped across to the opposite door. He knocked and listened; he brought his master-keys from his pocket. Expertly, he freed the bolt and peered in. The room was not occupied. He left the door ajar and returned to 1521.

MAKING SURE that he was not observed, Operator 5 carried Carrucci into the opposite room. Returning, he lifted Shepard Hunt carefully; he carried Hunt across the hall and placed him gently on the bed. Hunt was breathing laboriously, painfully. Operator 5 straightened as he heard quick footfalls in the hall, and glanced out to see Tim Donovan.

"In here, Tim!"

The boy slipped in, carrying a black leather case. Operator 5 closed the door tightly and snapped on the lights. For a long moment he bent to peer into Carrucci's face. He turned to a mirror, unfastened his collar, rolled up his sleeves, and opened the case. From it he took makeup materials.

He used them with consummate skill. A brown-toned liquid stained the skin of his face to a deeper shade. He worked with colorless spirit-gum and artificial hair to broaden and thicken his eyebrows. He applied tints carefully to shadow his eyes and mouth and again he applied stain. With carefully shaped wads of cotton, he changed the shape of his cheeks to the fullness of Carrucci's. He applied dark liquid to his hair which quickly dried, turning it black. He combed it in the manner of the unconscious man. Bit by bit, as Tim Donovan watched in amazement, his features underwent a weird change.

He turned and stripped off Carrucci's clothing. Ripping a pillowcase to strips, he bound Carrucci hand and foot. Removing his own suit, he donned that of the other man. He studied himself before the mirror, and turned to Tim.

The boy blurted excitedly: "You look just like him! If I hadn't seen it—!"

Operator 5 smiled grimly as he moistened his hands in the brown stain, applying it liberally to the eagle-shaped scar. He moved toward the bed on which Shepard Hunt lay. Hunt stirred with a moan and his eyes fluttered open. They widened in terror and he clutched the spread.

"Get away! By God, I'll kill—"

Operator 5 gripped Hunt's hand as it snatched at his throat. "Easy, Hunt!" His voice brought startled relief to Hunt's eyes. "You've uncovered the only possible lead to the Masked Power. No matter what you've been, you've cleared yourself. Thanks to you, I may be able to reach that man, and if I do—"

"Good luck!" burst from Hunt's numbed lips. "God, I wish you luck!"

Softly Operator 5 said: "Stout fellow, Hunt. You—careful!"

A spasm shook the pain-wracked body of Shepard Hunt. He straightened convulsively, his face twisting in agony. When he eased, his breath was beating rapidly, hotly. His hand sought Jimmy Christopher's and he gripped it fervently.

"Good luck!" he whispered huskily again. His eyes closed and be mumbled. Operator 5 bent close to hear; the whispered words brought grim darkness to his eyes! "Better—this way—Better than a—firing squad!"

The dead hand of Shepard Hunt dropped from Jimmy Christopher's grip.

Operator 5 rose slowly. Eyes glinting, he strode to the door and peered out. He signaled Tim Donovan after him into 1521. He made sure rapidly that the room showed no signs of the struggle. He tucked Carrucci's passport into his pocket as he spoke:

"Tim, you're going down. Stick with Dad. Tell Diane to join you once her man comes in. You're to watch the entrance—and if you see me going out, you're to follow in the roadster. Don't let anything stop you—it's the most important trail you've ever taken."

"Count on me, Jimmy!"

"I do! Listen. Once I reach my destination, leave Dad and Di and get as close to me as possible. Keep watch. If I'm able to do it, I'll pass you a message in some way. That message is to be relayed to Z-7 as fast as you can handle it. I may find myself in such a situation, Tim, that you'll be my only hope of sending a warning to the Chief."

A sharp ring of the telephone interrupted. Operator 5 spun to it. He lifted the receiver to hear Diane Elliot's voice:

"Jimmy! The other man is going up! He's on his way now!"

Operator 5 replaced the telephone hastily. "Outside, Tim! Join Dad and Di! There's no chance to tell you—" Operator 5 broke off, jerking open the door. "On your way, Tim!"

Jimmy Christopher thrust the boy through the door and immediately closed it. Tim Donovan turned quickly at the sound of the opening elevator grille. He saw a thick-bodied, sharp-eyed man alight and turn in his direction. At the first sound he had started forward. Now he strode on casually—past the man that came hurrying. He punched the elevator bell. A grille again opened as he saw the keen-eyed man pause at 1521 and knock. Tim Donovan stepped into the elevator with heart pounding heavily....

Inside 1521, the rap of knuckles echoed on the door. Operator 5 faced it grimly, hand on the knob. The man outside, he knew, was one who had known the real Carrucci, perhaps well.

The first glimpse of that man would be a test. If Operator 5's disguise failed to pass the scrutiny of Carrucci's friend, it meant that the one remaining lead to the Masked Power was blocked. His heart grew chilled as he twisted the knob and stepped back.

Into the room strode the thick-bodied man with piercing eyes. He closed the door behind him. He peered at Operator 5 intently, a hard smile on his lips.

"Carrucci!" he exclaimed. "You got my message? It's all arranged! I am going to take you to him! We must go together now—at once!"

CHAPTER 14
STEEL CLASHES STEEL

THE SEDAN traveled swiftly over the road that twined through hills banking the Hudson. Its curtains were drawn. At the wheel sat the agent of the Masked Power named Cupo; beside him, the man who was in appearance Raffaele Carrucci, in purpose and determination, Operator 5. Two hours ago they had left New York City; miles were flashing past swiftly. Somewhere out in this rolling country, Jimmy Christopher knew, must be a hiding place of the Masked Power.

He spoke little; he listened intently to Cupo's observations on the war, on the catastrophe planned to crush the United States. He had ordered Tim Donovan to follow with John Christopher and Diane; yet he had been able to catch no glimpse of any car following. He was left heart-heavy with dread that they had not been able to trace the sedan's swift course. Each added mile

179

was a torturous uncertainty to Operator 5, but he was forced to play his part to Cupo.

"But this man—who is he?" he asked.

"Never ask that!" Cupo snapped. "It is dangerous! Learn who he is, and you learn how to die! I have never seen his face—pray God I don't see it, even by accident, for that would mean the end of me. Ask no questions, Carrucci! Follow orders! His power is great—the greatest in the world!"

"And the pay is high!" Operator 5 said.

"High to those who serve him well. To those he does not trust—the pay is death!"

Cupo turned the car off the main highway, and sent it winding westward, through hills steeped in the darkness of night. Mile after mile flashed past, and still Operator 5 was unable to gain any assurance that his own roadster was following. He was forced to conclude that, if it was, Tim Donovan must be at the wheel, exerting all his skill at shadowing. Cupo continued to talk; the headlights continued to probe into darkness. The way led deep into lonely territory.

At last Cupo turned the car again, onto a narrow road. Presently it ran along an estate walled by a high hedge. It was in appearance a wealthy man's residence; there was, as the car approached the gate, no suggestion of suspicious activity about it. Behind the hedge, a fence stood; the gate was closed, but it was opened immediately by a man who appeared to be a caretaker. The car rolled toward a large house, sitting far back from the road, framed by broad grounds, and at the entrance it stopped.

Operator 5 paused. "Magnificent! This man is indeed one of position!"

Cupo laughed softly. "You see that large field there? It is a private airport. You cannot see the hangars, but a fleet of planes is kept in them. As for—listen!"

Out of the darkness beyond came a sudden metallic coughing sound that smoothed into a reverberating roar. "One of the planes is being warmed up!" Cupo exclaimed. "Perhaps it is for your use, Carrucci! A man of position? You see those masts rising over there? They support a wireless antenna. It is a licensed station. It receives messages from all over the world. There are private telephone lines and telegraph lines. He is in close touch with every capital. His word commands armies. You are fortunate, Carrucci—he selects his men with care!"

Operator 5 glanced back along the road as Cupo approached the door, hoping for a glimpse of his roadster, but there was none. After a moment of waiting, the door swung open. The man who appeared in the light seemed to be an impeccably liveried butler; but Jimmy Christopher noted a significant bulge at his hip, and scanned the cruel coldness of his eyes. They walked past him, into a sumptuously furnished library. There the butler bade them wait.

"I must warn you again! Complete silence! Complete obedience!" Cupo whispered.

A footfall sounded. The huge butler returned to the room and rumbled: "Mr. Carrucci—alone."

A NEW chill came to Operator 5's heart as he stepped forward. Cupo remained behind as he entered a long hallway. The butler preceded him with heavy step, past door after door. At the far end of the hall, they paused. The butler's huge hand opened a carved door. Operator 5 stepped through it, into a luxuriously furnished study. Behind him, the door clicked.

The room was empty. Near one side sat a carved desk, its top bare. Behind it, flush with the wall, gleamed the huge front of a safe. It was standing ajar a few inches; a light burning inside it sent a shaft into the room. Operator 5 advanced to the side of the desk, and stood smartly, waiting.

He saw the vault was lined with drawers, one of which was standing open, revealing files of papers inside. In the far wall was a device which he recognized as a ventilator. It was large and deep, a storehouse of records and wealth.

The soft sound of an opening door stirred the air of the room. Across the threshold stepped a huge man—his head enveloped in a black cowl. He paused, wordless, his gray eyes glinting through the slits in his hood, peering at Jimmy Christopher. They confronted each other silently a long moment—Operator 5 and the Masked Power.

The man in the mask strode briskly to the desk. He extended his hand and his husky voice came: "Your passport?"

Operator 5 promptly drew from his pocket the passport of Raffaele Carrucci and handed it across the desk. The masked man studied the photograph pasted inside it, and glanced keenly into Jimmy Christopher's disguised face. Long, tense moments passed before the Masked Power finished the comparison and tossed the passport to the desk.

"Very well," he said gratingly. "The man who brought you

here has already explained the necessity for absolute secrecy and loyalty. I do not intend to emphasize those points. Your failure to observe them will mean your instant death. Do you understand that fully?"

"I do, sir."

"Through others whom I trust," the Masked Power continued, "I have selected you for certain important tasks. You will begin your work immediately you leave this room. A plane is being made ready for you, and it is supplied with sufficient fuel so that you may reach the Mexican border without the necessity of stopping. Your task will be one which I have only now decided upon."

"I am ready for it, sir," Jimmy Christopher declared.

"Good. Listen carefully. Until tonight, my plans have moved forward without a halt. A step just taken by the United States government necessitates an important change. The invasion from Mexico until now was timed to occur at exactly noon tomorrow. I have already dispatched orders to my lieutenants in Mexico that the time for the invasion has been moved forward by hours. It will occur in the morning, at a time when the President of the United States will be reviewing his Tank Corps at Laredo."

A chill of apprehension passed through Jimmy Christopher's body.

"This move is calculated," the Masked Power continued levelly, "to give our forces the advantage of surprise. The United States tank defenses will be caught unawares. Our invasion will be already under way before the Army Command suspects it has started. Yet that is incidental to the main purpose for my change in plans. The strategy behind the move is, briefly, the death of the President of the United States."

OPERATOR 5 stood motionless, appalled by the revelation, coldly amazed at the man's calm tone.

"The assassination of the President will paralyze the government and terrorize the people. The shock of it will render them helpless. War will become absolutely inevitable—beyond the power of even one called Operator 5 to stop."

Jimmy Christopher's gaze sharpened on the gleaming eyes of the man in the mask. "Operator 5?" he exclaimed. "I have heard of him. You are afraid that—?"

"I fear nothing." Again the husky voice was heavily calm. "I know that Operator 5 is bent on keeping the United States out of war. I realize that, due to certain facts he has learned, which he intends to lay before the world, he might succeed. The death of the President of the United States will make his success impossible. The assassination of the Chief Executive will arouse public terror which will drive the United States into the war. You are to strike that blow!"

Operator 5 blurted: "I?"

"You—yes!" The Masked Power quickly opened the drawer of the desk and placed on the top of it a number of documents banded together. "Your instructions are to fly directly to the field at Laredo. These papers will identify you as a citizen of the United States and as a member of the United States Intelligence Service. With them are forged orders instructing you to act as a bodyguard for the President while he reviews the Tank Corps. You will not be questioned; you will kill him!"

Jimmy Christopher's lips pressed hard.

"Yet do not think," the Masked Power continued, "that I am relying entirely upon you to accomplish this purpose. My orders to the commanders of the invading tanks have directed them to concentrate a drive upon the field at Laredo. Those tanks will move so swiftly that the field will be surrounded before the United States Army officers there realize what is happening. The tank guns will be able to reach the spot on which the President stands. Should your gun not reach him, Carrucci, the President will find escape impossible by ground or air. He will be trapped—he will certainly die!"

"I understand!"

"Thus the assassination of the President is doubly assured," the Masked Power continued. "It will demoralize the Army Command. Our tank units will have already begun an advance which will carry them far across the border. We will seize all United States defenses as we advance, and with them, hold the territory we conquer. Thus the revolutionist leaders of the invasion will be rewarded, and thus the United States will find itself plunged headlong into the war with utter destruction and inevitability."

The Masked Power leaned forward. "There can be no delay. It is late. You have just time enough for the flight to Laredo. You will take off at once, with my best pilot. By the time you reach the field, the President will be reviewing the Tank Corps. Your mission will take but a few minutes, and then—"

185

The rasp of a buzzer broke into the words of the Masked Power. He ceased speaking and touched the cam of a dictaphone set in the open desk drawer. A voice twanged out: "Necessary to see you at once, sir!"

"Very well. Come in." And to Jimmy Christopher, he bade: "Wait!"

OUTSIDE THE door footfalls sounded. It opened to admit the man whom Operator 5 had seen at the gate. In the gloom, he had appeared to be an old caretaker; now, in the brighter light, he was revealed as a young man of powerful physical strength, with a sharp, cruel face. In one hand he was gripping a huge automatic. He advanced and exclaimed: "We've caught a prowler, sir!"

"A prowler?" the masked man echoed.

"We found him hiding near the side of the house! He must have climbed over the fence, sir. He was trying to get near the window of this room, sir, apparently in order to listen to what was being said. He tried to escape, but we have him!"

"Bring him in!"

The sentry turned smartly to the door. He snapped a command that brought two other men into the light. They advanced holding the arms of their prisoner—a boy. Operator 5 saw his pinched face, his widened eyes. It was Tim!

Tim Donovan peered at Operator 5—and away again. No sign of recognition came into his eyes. He squirmed to escape the men who held him—fought hopelessly. They dragged him forward as Jimmy Christopher stared in frozen consternation. The boy had been captured because he had followed orders to approach Operator 5's destination as close as possible—of that Jimmy Christopher was certain. The realization dazed him as he stepped aside, striving his utmost to hide his fear.

Through the slits in the black cowl the eyes of the Masked Power brightened. He straightened, and a hard chuckle came from his hidden lips. He declared:

"I know this boy. He is a friend of Operator 5. He has been assisting Operator 5 in the work against me. You have done well to capture him!"

"He was alone, sir!" the sentry blurted.

"You're positive of that?" the man in the mask demanded. "You're positive that Operator 5 is not also on the grounds?"

"We searched, sir, thinking there might be someone with him. We're certain there is no one else. He came here alone!"

The man in the cowl leaned across the desk, peering into Tim Donovan's white face. "Where is Operator 5?"

Tim Donovan faced the Masked Power defiantly. His small hands formed into fists and his eyes flared. "I won't tell you!"

The husky voice came again. "Consider well, young man. One word from me, and you will be killed." I will grant you life only if you answer my questions. *Where is—Operator 5?*"

The tough Irish lad stood silent.

The Masked Power straightened. "In the rear of this house," he declared in his rasping voice, "there is a room which is perfectly soundproofed. The reports of the guns that shoot you down will be inaudible beyond those walls. Far back on my grounds there is a plot of earth where dead men lie. You will be buried beside them unless you choose to talk."

Tears glistened in Tim Donovan's eyes but he spoke grimly: "You can't make me say anything!"

The Masked Power continued. "There is another room which you will see first. Have you ever heard of the rack? Do you know that men who lie upon it, being slowly pulled limb from limb, feeling their muscles tearing apart, often change their minds about talking? You will find it far pleasanter to speak now, before you are taken into that room."

JIMMY CHRISTOPHER peered, chilled with horror, into the blazing eyes of Tim Donovan. The boy stood with small fists still clenched, gazing fearlessly at the man in the cowl. "You can't make me say anything!"

The Masked Power straightened and gestured to his sentries. "Take him away! Put him on the rack. Do not spare him!"

The men gripping Tim Donovan's arms jerked him back. Operator 5's haggard gaze followed him toward the door, but the boy did not glance back. Shoulders squared, chin lifted, he passed into the hallway beyond. The door closed; there was no sound save the beating of heels moving away.

Operator 5 glanced around quickly. The room was closed. He faced the Masked Power alone. He stepped forward grimly, peering at the metallic gray eyes of the cowled man.

"I was informing you, Carrucci, that you will begin at once to fly—"

Jimmy Christopher interrupted sharply: "It is not necessary that you torture a boy! That is too much!"

The Masked Power stiffened. "You disapprove? You dare to—?"

"A word from you will stop it now!"

"A word from me," the Masked Power declared slowly, "is sufficient to cause the death of anyone who dares interfere. Take care, Carrucci!"

Operator 5 leaned forward grimly. "You wished to know," he said levelly, "the whereabouts of Operator 5. That is your purpose in torturing the boy. Perhaps you will countermand your order if I give you that information?"

Through the slits of his cowl, the eyes of the Masked Power narrowed. "What! You know where Operator 5 is?"

"I do!" Jimmy Christopher's right hand grew tense. "He is standing before you!" His fingers flashed inside his coat. A motion too rapid for the eye to follow brought his arm-pitted automatic into his hand. It flashed level; it peered darkly across the desk at the huge masked man. The man in the cowl straightened slowly, never glancing at the gun, peering intently into Jimmy Christopher's face.

"You *are* Operator 5!"

Operator 5's voice rang. "Use that dictaphone! Call the room where those men have taken Tim Donovan. Order them to bring him back!"

"That I decline to do!" A throaty chuckle came from the black cowl. "You are aiming, I see, directly at my heart. It is your intention to fire if I do not obey your orders. You ought to realize, Operator 5, that I do not fear your bullet. I am a man of steel—steel protects me."

Jimmy Christopher remained quiet.

"You may empty your gun point-blank at me," the Masked

Operator 5 commanded sharply: "Order your men to release Tim Donovan!"

Power said slowly, "and I will not be harmed. My body is completely covered by a bulletproof garment of steel mesh. My mask is lined with it. If you shoot straight at my head, the bullets will be turned away by it. Your gun cannot possibly hurt me."

Operator 5 kept it level.

"Your attempt to save your friend," the Masked Power continued gratingly, "is futile. I admire your courage—but you have revealed yourself in vain. You have made yourself a prisoner here and you will find escape impossible. You will see that room to which your friend was taken! You will learn what pain is! You will die in agony beside him!"

CHAPTER 15
THE GODS DEAL A HAND!

THE HAND of the Masked Power reached toward the dictaphone in the drawer. Instantly Jimmy Christopher stepped back. He dropped his automatic and with the same movement gripped the buckle of his belt. A sharp swing of his arm jerked it from its loops; the thin leather scabbard flew from the long, glittering blade of his rapier. He flashed the supple steel downward and its razor-sharp edge whipped across the Masked Power's hand.

Blood spurted. The cowled man jerked back in sudden fury. Jimmy Christopher slipped swiftly around the desk, his rapier flashing in the light. The point flicked to the mask which covered the big man's head. It darted beneath the edge of the black, steel-lined fabric. It poised, vibrating, needle-sharp, pricking the skin of the Masked Power's neck.

The man in the mask stiffened. Operator 5 took a quick step closer, gripping the hilt of the rapier, keeping its point in position—and he smiled: "You are a man of steel," he said coldly, "and at this moment you face death by steel. One slight move of my hand and this blade will pierce your throat. You will fall before you can utter a cry for help. Your protection against bullets is not of the slightest help to you now. I suggest that you listen and follow orders!"

The Masked Power stood rigid as a statue, trembling with fury, frozen by the sharp touch of the rapier point on his throat, his metallic eyes glinting.

Operator 5 commanded sharply: "Now, speak through your instrument! Call your torture room! Order your men to release Tim Donovan! Unless you do—!"

One long moment, the Masked Man stood motionless. Slowly, then, his great hand reached toward the dictaphone in the desk drawer. Operator 5, withdrawing cautiously, kept the point of the rapier poised as the man in the cowl moved forward. The fingers touched the cam; an answering voice rasped into the room.

"I—I have changed my mind. Release the boy!"

"Release him?" rattled from the instrument. "Yes, sir!"

Jimmy Christopher whispered tensely: "He is to be returned to the door of this room—no farther!"

The Masked Power harshly echoed the instructions. "Bring him back to the door of my study and hold him there!"

"He is," Operator 5 demanded softly, "to be placed in my custody."

Into the instrument the Masked Power declared: "My lieutenant, Carrucci, is to take charge of him. Carrucci has his orders. Follow them strictly."

"That is all," Operator 5 whispered.

The Masked Power tipped the cam back. When he straightened the needle-pointed *épée* remained poised at his throat. Jimmy Christopher, his eyes gleaming, faced the cowled man with a tight smile. "Now," he commanded, "open the door of the vault. Go into it!"

Slowly, step after step, the man in the cowl retreated toward the huge door of the vault. His great hands swung it wide open as Operator 5 followed, every muscle tense, the rapier never wavering. Into the brighter light of the vault, the Masked Power retreated. They paused there.

"You once said," Jimmy Christopher declared softly, "that a glimpse of your face means death. I'll take a chance."

His left hand reached forward quickly; he gripped the edge of the cowl and jerked it high. Blackness vanished from the face of the Power; his features were revealed in bright light. Operator 5 stood motionless, studying the man's face—a large face, graven with deep, black lines. The metallic eyes glistened with consummate wrath; the cruel mouth pressed hard. It was a mask of mercilessness.

"Barton Hildreth," Operator 5 said quietly. "International banker. Stock manipulator. United States citizen and one of the richest men in the world. You kept your face masked because one glimpse of it would have betrayed your false leadership of the Secret League!"

Barton Hildreth's icy eyes flashed their threats. Operator 5 looked right and left. He reached out toward a telephone sitting on a shelf; he flung it back, and its cord ripped free. He retreated a step, still keeping the rapier poised, its point resting on Barton Hildreth's throat.

"You will not be able to call for help over that telephone now. I believe, Mr. Hildreth, that no one knows the combination of this vault but you? While you remain here you will, of course, be perfectly safe."

He reached again, to a switch set in the wall. Above it were two circular openings in a plate of metal. A turn of the switch caused leaves to fall back within the wall of the vault, opening two tubes that penetrated through the steel and concrete. At the same time a contact closed; an electric fan, also concealed behind the panel, began to *whirr*. Into the closed space air began to pour in through the ventilator.

"A wise precaution, Mr. Hildreth," Operator 5 said quietly. "You need not fear suffocation. You will not find it at all uncomfortable as long as the ventilator functions. I bid you—goodnight!"

Jimmy Christopher stepped backward swiftly. A sharp thrust, and the heavy steel slab swung into place. It thumped shut in its frame; the great bolts sank into their sockets. A twist of Operator 5's fingers spun the combination dial. He made sure that the vault was sealed—that the revealed Power was imprisoned beyond rescue or escape—and turned.

Quickly he sheathed his rapier, curled it around his waist, and buckled the belt-clasp. He slipped his automatic into his armpit holster. He listened sharply, sensed a movement beyond the door. He stepped toward it and gripped the knob. He flung it wide, and in the hallway, saw Tim Donovan standing guarded by the men who captured him.

The boy's eyes pleaded with Operator 5. Jimmy Christopher peered at him with simulated coldness as he spoke to the sentries.

"You have been informed that this boy is to remain in my custody? I am instructed to make use of the plane which is now ready for me. I will leave at once, and this boy will accompany me. He is not armed? Then tie his wrists!"

The man of powerful frame, garbed as the caretaker, hesitated uncertainly. "This is most unusual. The master must verify the orders he gave over the wire. I must see him and—"

"He has given you orders! Do you dare question them?" Operator 5 demanded angrily. "Waste no time! Do not meddle and upset our carefully laid plans! Tie the boy—and we'll go to the plane!"

Immediately the men gripping Tim Donovan's arms jerked him toward the rear of the huge house. Operator 5 strode briskly behind him. They paused in a small room, and the caretaker brought a length of thin rope. He whipped it about Tim Donovan's wrists. Again they moved along the hallway, to a heavy door at its rear end. The caretaker opened it, and cold night air gusted inside.

"The plane is directly ahead, sir, across the field. The pilot is waiting. We will—"

"You will go no farther with us! I have the boy well in hand. That is all!"

Jimmy Christopher seized one of Tim Donovan's arms. Through the darkness he could see, dimly, the outlines of a cabin plane waiting on the field, flame gushing from its exhaust stacks. Toward it he marched the tough Irish lad.

"Keep up the play, Tim!" he whispered. "We won't be safe until—"

A voice, speaking suddenly near the rear entrance of the house, broke out:

"The Master—where is he? He is not in the study! He is not anywhere! I can't find him! There are important dispatches and—who is that leaving?"

"By God!" the caretaker's voice burst. "Something's wrong! Stop that man! Keep him from reaching the plane!"

Operator 5 whirled. His hand flashed to his armpit holster as he glimpsed the four men sprinting toward him. He whispered, "To the plane, Tim! Make it fast!" and brought his weapon level. Swiftly he fired—four times. The bullets whined through the darkness and clicked into the wall behind the running men. Startled shouts broke from their lips and they scattered in alarm.

Jimmy Christopher swung to follow the running boy. Tim was sprinting toward the waiting plane with all the speed he could muster. Behind, in the darkness, continued movements sounded and a gun barked. Three slugs whirred across the open space as Operator 5 and Tim Donovan hastened.

"Call the others!" a voice bellowed. "Guard the roads! Stop them!"

A dark figure blocked the door of the cabin plane as Jimmy Christopher sped toward it. The uniformed pilot ducked out; a metallic glitter in his hand told that he was bringing an automatic into play. It swung toward Operator 5 as they leaped nearer. Swiftly Jimmy Christopher fired again. Straight to the pilot's gun the slugs sped.

The pilot sprawled backward with a howl of rage, the weapon torn from his fingers by the power of Jimmy Christopher's slugs. Operator 5 whipped about and again sent warning bullets crashing across the open space. "In, Tim!" he commanded and backed to the cabin door. As the boy scrambled through, he leaped inside and swung the door shut.

He shouldered into the control pit, dropped to the seat. He threw off the brakes and thrust the throttle wide. Roaring power surged from the motor; the propeller became a blur; flame flowed more brightly from the exhaust stacks. Jimmy Christopher sent the crate rolling swiftly across the field while the barking of guns echoed. A window of the cabin shattered at the impact of a bullet; another slug pierced the wall. Operator 5 whipped the plane about to send it plunging into the take-off.

Thunder shook the sky as he brought the crate into a swift climb. Tim Donovan scrambled beside him as the wings leveled. Operator 5, one hand freed, brought a knife from his pocket; its blade bore against Tim Donovan's bonds.

"Jimmy—look!" the boy blurted. "There're lights on the roads! Those men're getting close to Dad and Di!"

"Where are they, Tim?" Jimmy Christopher asked. "They don't know—"

"Below—Jimmy! Off the side of the road! They're waiting there!"

Operator 5 flung the plane into another bank. He peered down into the dark lane of the road twining through the hills. Tim gave quick directions as he swung low. Along the road, torches were flashing as men ran with them. Farther beyond, a bright gleam shone—the headlamps of a car speeding from the Masked Power's estate, hurtling into a chase of the plane. The shafting beams flickered upon a car drawn off the pavement—a roadster.

Operator 5 cut the gun and sent the plane plunging. He weaved it down between lanes of tall trees, into the danger of a brush against the branches that would crash the crate to earth. Plying the controls gingerly, he dropped closer and closer to the pavement. The trucks touched; the tail slapped down. Operator 5 thrust the brakes hard as Tim Donovan scrambled back to the cabin door.

"Dad!" the boy screeched. "Di! Quick! In here!"

The lights were playing more brightly on the roadster as its door flew open. John Christopher ducked out of it; Diane Elliot hurried from the farther side. Guns barked beyond, and bullets whistled along the road as they reached the door of the plane. They climbed in breathlessly and the door slammed shut.

Operator 5 sent the plane zooming. The motor beat power into the quiet of the night sky as he reached clearer air.

Sparkling lights twinkled away behind him as he reached

toward a shortwave radio installation in the control compartment. He snapped on the tubes. While they warmed, he smiled reassurance at John Christopher and Diane. Tim Donovan crowded in beside him anxiously.

"Good boy, Tim!" he exclaimed. "Not even the rack would have made you talk! Good boy!"

Tim smiled at the compliment. "You took an awful chance, yourself!" he said.

Operator 5, nudging the controls, quickly brought a pair of 'phones to his ears. "Calling M-9! Calling M-9! No distorter! Operator 5 calling M-9!"

Suddenly a voice burst in his ears. "M-9 answering! We've got you!"

"Bring Z-7 to the microphone!" Operator 5 commanded imperatively. "Z-7!"

A tight moment passed. A sputtering crackle sounded in Operator 5's ears. Then, through the background noises, the Washington Chief responded.

"Operator 5, Chief! Important information! I have made the Masked Power a prisoner. Note the location! Send all the men you can spare. Hold that place! More important than that, Chief, are orders to be transmitted to the Secret Service men detailed to guard the President tomorrow morning!

"No man who is not personally known to the President is to be allowed near him! A plan is in operation to assassinate him! The tank invasion has been directed to concentrate its force upon Laredo and trap him in a double effort to bring about his death. More than that the invasion has been ordered for the very time when the President will be reviewing the Tank Corps tomorrow morning!"

Z-7 blurted: "We'll take every precaution!"

"Were my orders transmitted to the Commander at Laredo? Is the sprayer-plane made ready?"

"Yes."

"We must have others, Chief! The change in the plan of invasion makes that absolutely necessary. You must flash every airfield along the border immediately, repeating to the Commanders the formula for the mixture I have already given you. They are to prepare planes exactly like the one waiting at Laredo. Sprayers must be rushed to the fields which do not have them now. The best pilots available must be assigned to those ships. When the signal comes, they are to take off and let nothing stop them from spraying the enemy tanks with the mixture!"

"I will send those orders at once! The War Department has organized a force which is treating all goggles on hand with Dicyanin A. Three factories at scattered points are working under full force turning out new ones. We are dispatching shipments of them by plane to all Tank Corps and Air Corps headquarters along the Border. Where are you, Operator 5? Where are you now?"

"In the air, Chief!" Operator 5 spoke briskly as he sent the plane plunging at top speed. "I'm bound for Laredo!"

CHAPTER 16
BATTLE OF THE MONSTERS

A CROSS THE night sky, Operator 5 kept the cabin crate traveling at the limit of its power. Black hours flashed past. Out of the east came the first golden light of the dawn, to stream its colors across the zenith, to brighten swiftly into the new day. The rising sun shafted long shadows across flat, open territory. Tense at the controls, with Tim Donovan at his side, with John Christopher and Diane Elliot anxiously watching him, Operator 5 sped over a crow's course toward the point of threatened attack.

Far beneath the plane, as the sun mounted, rolled desert wilderness. Below stretched vast expanses of sand carpeted with brown and green mesquite.

Out of the vast desert appeared the oasis of a settlement. In the bright sunlight, the town of Laredo materialized. Beyond it Fort Roosevelt came into view. Operator 5 peered into rolling territory where army maneuvers might take place unseen across the Rio; he detected no movement. Directly he drove for the fort, where the widely heralded review of the new United States Tank Corps units was being held.

Operator 5 peered with admiration on the display. Gleaming in the sun, hundreds of the new fast tanks were parading. In formation, giant crawling weapons of war, they were streaming from the roads and shifting into broader ranks to pass the Headquarters building. There on the steps, men were standing, watching the exhibition of the defensive strength of the Border.

Among those men, Jimmy Christopher knew, was the President of the United States.

He drove swiftly toward an open space beyond the operations building. There he saw an Army pursuit waiting. Its lines revealed that it was new, one of the swiftest models ever developed for the Air Corps. Toward it Operator 5 drove the cabin job, spiraling low. As he descended, uniformed men ran into the open. Jimmy Christopher saw them watching alertly as he brought the trucks of his crate down to the smooth field.

He trundled toward them and applied the brakes. As he opened the door, the officers sprang close. Their hands were ready on their service guns. Operator 5's swarthy skin, the artificially foreign cast of his features, struck them with suspicion. He paused to peer at the ranks of gleaming tanks rattling across the vast field, then stepped toward a man wearing the decorations of a captain.

"Who are you, sir? It is forbidden—"

Operator 5 quickly removed a thin silver case from his pocket. A touch on a concealed spring, and its cover flew up, revealing a document framed inside. He proffered it to the captain, and the amazed officer broke off to read the few lines on the paper inside:

THE WHITE HOUSE
Washington

To Whom It May Concern:
The identity of the bearer of this letter must be kept strictly confidential.

He is Operator 5 of the United States Intelligence Service.

The name signed to the document was that of the President of the United States.

"I must see the President at once!" Operator 5 declared.

"Certainly, sir! Follow me!"

"I shall want the use of that plane immediately!"

"It is ready, sir!"

JIMMY CHRISTOPHER strode smartly toward the Headquarters building. Past it, the long ranks of tanks were clattering, reflecting the sun, moving into maneuvers of amazing agility. On the steps of the operations building, a crowd of army officers and state dignitaries were watching. Sound motion-picture cameras were recording the scene; newspaper photographers were busy. Up the steps, with the Captain, Operator 5 mounted, toward the tall, dignified man in their midst.

The President peered at him quizzically. Jimmy Christopher stepped close to whisper: "Operator 5, sir."

The amazement of the Chief Executive passed. "I would never have recognized you! This is the first opportunity I have had to congratulate you on the successful completion of your mission to Balkaria. It is impossible for me to express my gratitude—but thank God we have you in the service!"

"Thank you, Mr. President," Operator 5 answered tightly. His voice was low, inaudible to the officers standing close. "Z-7 has warned you of the danger here. I have learned that the proposed invasion is to strike at an earlier hour. You must leave the fort as soon as possible!"

Operator 5 broke off as a uniformed man hurried from the

door of the Headquarters building to the step and snapped a salute. His breathless words, addressed to the Major-General commanding the post carried to every man on the steps.

"Radio from our patrol planes, sir! They have sighted enemy tanks moving toward the Border! Hundreds of them are advancing to cross the line!"

Operator 5 whirled to face the Chief Executive. "The invasion has begun!"

Consternation brought dark lines into the faces of the officers who heard. The President turned to face the Major-General. His voice was tight, crisp, commanding. "Give your orders, General!"

Jimmy Christopher's hand closed about the Commander's arm.

"Order your tanks to surround this field! They must keep the invading tanks away from it at all costs! Send your other units ahead to block the enemy advance! They are concentrating their forces toward this spot! Lose no time!"

Operator 5 spun off the steps. He hurried past the Headquarters building toward the plane waiting for him. Tim Donovan was standing beside it; John Christopher and Diane Elliot were waiting with him. He reached inside the pit for helmet and goggles.

"In the rear cubby, Tim! I need you. Dad—take your place with the President. Do your best to get him off this field as soon as possible. Di—Lord, you've got to leave at once!"

Diane Elliot's eyes were gleaming. "I'm a reporter—I belong here! I'll be all right! I'll stick with Dad and—"

From the south boomed reports that trembled through the

earth and shook the sky. Through the air sounded the shrill scream of flying shells. Invisible death in the sunlight, the small projectiles streaked through their trajectories, each emitting a shrill whine that pierced the ears. A moment of tension, of stunned inaction, struck the field—then the concussions were echoed by a rending force that descended to the earth.

Fire roared high! Smoke gushed from craters created in the sand of the field. Flying dirt darkened the sun. At scattered points on the field, the shells struck with rending violence. Sand scattered over the moving tanks. Fumes whipped away on the wind to disclose four of them tumbled on their sides, the others scattering swiftly from the pitfalls. And into the rumbling echoes snapped the sharp commands of frantic officers.

The guns of the invading tanks—engines of war still invisible—had opened fire!

OPERATOR 5 gripped the cowling of the plane as pungent smoke washed across it. Tim Donovan clambered frantically into the pit behind him. He settled to the controls as a mechanic rushed to whip the prop over. The hot engine burst into a roar as booming reports again shook the distant air. Desperately Operator 5 called: "To the President, Dad!" and threw off the brakes.

He sent the crate streaking across the field while a sandstorm whipped behind its propeller. He flung it into the takeoff and dared a low bank that sent him back toward the headquarters buildings. The parade ground was pocked by the shells that had fallen. The black masses of the speed-tanks were driving in a swift maneuver, flinging their flanks toward the edges of the

From the tail of the speeding plane, the black rain descended.

206

It spattered the monsters crawling along the Rio Grande river bed!

field. Near the high gate, fire flamed in the sunlight and black smoke gushed over broken ground.

Several of the shells had fallen among the automobiles stationed there. Laden with up-thrown sand, turned on their sides, wiped by flames torn in the wind, transformed into misshapen masses of metal, they jolted with the force of another shell that plunged into their midst even as Operator 5 watched. One of those cars had carried the President to the scene. Men, hurrying toward the spot where destruction had blasted, backed away from the terrific heat of the burning gasoline. One of them gestured frantically to the President, waving him back, as Operator 5 whirled overhead.

The road leading to the gate was deeply pitted. Craters and up-thrown earth made it impassable. Grimly, Operator 5 realized that the first blast of the attack had doubly destroyed the means of removing the Chief Executive from the focus of danger. He hastily snapped the switch of his plane's radio equipment and affixed headphones and microphone. Immediately the tubes heated, his sharp voice carried orders, through the ether.

"Calling Fort Roosevelt! Relay orders for planes to come to your field. The President must be removed at once! Continue the tank maneuver to surround the fort!"

Quickly, as he sent his plane howling toward the south, he trimmed the oscillator to a shorter wavelength. Again he spoke quickly into the microphone: "Calling all airfields along the Border! Calling all United States Border Patrol fields! The sprayer planes are to take off at once! Operate directly above the invading tanks! Make sure you touch none of our tanks! Top speed!"

Around Fort Roosevelt, the swift-moving metal monsters spread, as Operator 5 droned toward the Border. He flashed above the dry bed of the Rio Grande—peered down at a scene which struck his heart cold. Massing below were other tanks, glistening black mammoths of swift pace and crushing power, their guns waving like poisonous antennae—the tanks of the revolutionist invaders!

Operator 5 flung his plane directly above them. Below, guns roared and shells screamed upward, reaching for his wings. One hit by a projectile, Operator 5 realized, was sufficient to strike him from the sky, to utterly destroy the strategy upon which all hope of repulsing the invasion depended. He sent the plane plunging above the black-backed engines of war, flying low, rocking from wing to wing.

"Ready, Tim!" he called through the roar of the motor. "Pull that lever!"

Tim Donovan twined both hands about the control of the spraying device mounted in the rear pit. He threw it into the open position with all his strength. The power of the exhaust surged through the instrument, and a loud hissing mingled with the beating of the engine. From the tail of the speeding plane a black rain began to descend.

It pelted down upon the enemy tanks massing at the banks of the Rio and crawling across its bed. Black drops sprinkled over the shining metal, becoming almost invisible against it. Desperately, Operator 5 rocked his crate, weaving back and forth above the invading forces, while Tim Donovan held the sprayer unit open.

OPERATOR 5 shouted into his microphone: "Calling Fort Roosevelt! Relay orders to all airfields and Tank Corps! All pilots and tank crews are to wear the special goggles!"

From the antenna of the Fort Roosevelt radio station, the orders flashed along the Border. Into the rumbling, cluttering interiors of the tanks, the orders echoed. Into the pits of battle planes flinging off the fields of scattered Air Corps posts, the words reached. In the sky and on the earth, men obeyed. And as their eyes became accustomed to the color of the Dicyanin A, they witnessed a transformation the like of which they had never seen before.

Tanks crawling spattered with spots that glowed! A ghostly shine emanating from raindrops of black! Up from the valley of the Rio, masses of the marked tanks appeared, clearly distinguishable from the United States machines of war that rushed to meet their advance. The enemy crates were branded!

"Watch your fire!" the radioed voice rang inside the tanks and in the pits of flocking airplanes. "Fire only on tanks spotted with the glowing mixture! They are the invaders! Tanks not marked are ours! The enemy crews cannot discern this difference! Maneuver not only to block their way but close in behind them! Take advantage of their confusion!"

Far up the course of the Rio, Operator 5 flung his crate, darting deep into the sand hills, swerving along the banks crawling with the enemy tanks, twisting above American soil to drench an advancing black line of revolutionist war engines. Every muscle alert, his eyes darting to every speeding mass, he swung low while the black rain dropped. Far up the course of the Rio, until he saw another swift army pursuit traveling in his direction, likewise pouring its mixture from the sky. Then, swiftly, he banked and drove back.

Operator 5 kept his radial wide open as he howled back along the weaving line of the Rio. Into the sky above him were swarming squadrons of battle planes from the Border fields. From the south swarmed crates flown by revolutionists. Combat ships whipped about combat ships as savage dogfights broke out above the Rio. American bombers streaked low as observers released trips that sent vaned projectiles plunging down upon the enemy tanks still streaming toward the Border.

With amazing swiftness, the armored tanks darted through their maneuvers, seeking advances, repulsing concerted drives, blasting their guns against steel-plate walls. Into the midst of the enemy flanks, bombs streaked, tossing the hostile tanks into fuming craters. Mile after mile of the Border saw the fury of the weird battle that rose to a desperate pitch as swift black lines of crawling monsters met.

Plunging into view of Fort Roosevelt, Operator 5 saw a plane whirling above it. It was, he knew, one of the ships responding to his order, a plane whose pilot was intent upon removing the President from the focus of the attack. In the air about it, black bursts appeared as shells exploded, as the invading tanks strove to reach it with their guns. It whipped through clouds of vapor, rocking on punctured wings. It swerved to dart down to the field and doom struck it!

Into the very heart of the streaking plane, a shell from an enemy tank plunged. Instantly flames enveloped it; instantly it was a plunging mass of destruction. It swerved swiftly until its motor choked off; it spilled wing over wing, plunging into the open desert. Operator 5's grim eyes followed it until he saw it strike the sand and disintegrate into a mass of flaming debris— its pilot dead amidst it.

NO OTHER plane was near the field. Jimmy Christopher banked swiftly, directly toward it. On the ground below, a black ring had formed around Fort Roosevelt, a circle of United States tanks whose guns were blasting at enemies advancing all around. Within the fence of the fort, the field lay pitted and heaped. Near the operations building, officers stood guard with side-arms and rifles. Beside the offices, a narrow strip lay untouched by the falling shells. On it sat the cabin plane. Operator 5 drove his crate toward it as the air shook with the concussions of savage explosions.

Tim Donovan clung to the cowling, the sprayer unit shut off, as Operator 5 side-slipped over the fence. The trucks of the crate slashed through loose sand. Hard-jammed brakes smoked. The plane ran close beside the cabin job in which Operator 5 had flown to the fort. He leaped out and Tim Donovan scrambled after him as he ran to the Headquarters building.

He shouldered past white-faced officers, thrust through a door, and came to a stop facing the President.

"The enemy tanks are directing their shells into the field more heavily every moment. They will certainly strike this building very soon. Your only chance is to leave the fort by air. It's dangerous, sir—but to remain here would be fatal. If you will permit me to pilot you—?"

Terrific force struck the field again; two shells, falling together, thrust their power into the earth. Blinding sand flew. The windows of the operations office shattered outward. The shock stirred the walls and brought dismayed exclamations from the officers inside. Operator 5's hand seized the President's arm. "At once, sir!"

Officers marched with the President to the door. Jimmy Christopher's glance signaled his father and Diane Elliot to follow. He strode upon a field gusting with the pungent fumes of explosives. As the President hurried toward the waiting cabin plane, another rending shock tore across the field and through the air came the scream of shells reaching in ever increasing numbers toward the fort.

The Chief Executive hurried into the cabin. Operator 5 helped Diane through the door. Tim Donovan and John Christopher ducked in. Jimmy Christopher sidled into the control compartment as officers hastened to the wings. They tailed the ship about hastily. One of them seized the crank of the engine. Again the earth shook with the power of exploding shells and a blast of sand washed across the plane.

"For God's sake, take it up!" an officer screeched. "Get away from this field! They'll try to pick you off once—!"

The engine thundered. Operator 5 threw off the brakes. He tensed at the controls as the plane shot across a field made treacherous by loose sand. With all the ability at his command, he kept it running true; then he felt its tail lift. Desperately, he flung it into the air as mound-rimmed craters cut off the way. It roared up, circling sharply, driving toward the north, and the air turned black around it with the poisonous fumes of hostile shells.

The rocking blasts of the shells passed behind. The air grew clearer. The radial roared with a steady, powerful song. Operator 5 glanced back, into air blackened by battle, as he drove out of the area of conflict. He raised, smiling, and through the open door called back: "We're clear, sir!"

The President's answer was audible only to Diane Elliot while the motor continued to blast: "Knowing you, Operator 5, I had no fear that we would not come clear!"

In the control compartment, Operator 5 affixed the 'phones of the radio equipment. Carefully, as he sent the plane climbing, he trimmed the receiver to the shortwave bands used by the army posts along the border. He caught voices out of the ether—reports to Washington.

"The tank invasion is stopped at El Paso! El Paso reporting the invasion stopped! We have the situation in hand. Thanks to the glow-mixture and the special goggles, we were able—"

Another voice: "Fort Roosevelt attack subsiding. Our tanks are advancing, repulsing the enemy! Hundreds of the hostile tanks are turning back toward the Rio! Our bombers are driving back those which have not yet crossed!"

And, sounding far away, another voice sang through the air: "For God's sake, reach the President! Congress is already acting upon the news of the invasion! A declaration of war can only be averted by a message from the President! We must have news from him!"

Operator 5's gesture brought the Chief Executive into the control compartment. The President affixed the ear-'phones; he listened intently to a repetition of the message. Into the microphone, his words ran: "The President is speaking! I am returning to Washington now! Congress must be told that a declaration of war is impossible! I will appear before them as soon as I return!"

Across the spreading wilderness of sand, Jimmy Christopher flung the plane at its limit of speed. Washington, and the salvation of the United States from the destruction of war, lay ahead!

CHAPTER 17
SHEATHED SWORDS

ACROSS THE United States flashed news that heartened a terrorized people:

Invasion from Mexico Repulsed!
Attacks Stopped on All Fronts!
Our Tank Units Command the Border!
War Danger Stamped Out!
President Demands Peace!

Over nationwide radio broadcasts additional details carried to relieved millions:

"The President, appearing before Congress immediately after he returned to Washington by air, declared that the United States must not enter the war. His command of the situation was swiftly taken. The United States government is determined to keep out of the conflict!

"Immediately after his speech to Congress, the President closeted himself with the Ambassadors of all warring nations. A momentous conference is taking place at this moment. Its import is of worldwide significance, it is known, but the result cannot be guessed. The entire United States is watching the conference now taking place in the White House!"

The nation waited—and Operator 5 followed the leads of the gravest case he had ever handled. In a sedan, with Z-7 and Tim Donovan beside him, he went that night to the isolated house in the hills beyond New York which had served as a headquarters for the Masked Power. He found Intelligence men in charge of it. They had made prisoners of Barton Hildreth's lieutenants; they had kept the house under guard. With Tim Donovan and Z-7 at his side, Operator 5 strode along the corridor toward the study.

He entered it and paused, peering at the black front of the vault. He stepped into the adjoining room, seeking the outlets of the ventilator. He gazed coldly at the metal plate in the wall, with its two openings, and a dark glitter came into his eyes. He returned slowly to the front of the vault while Z-7 stood by anxiously.

"It will take some time, Chief," he said quietly. "We'll have to use torches unless I can find the combination…."

He stripped off his coat and rubbed his fingertips on the blotter of the desk, felt them gingerly. He advanced to the safe and began slowly turning the combination dial. His sensitive fingers poised delicately; his lids lowered; he worked with silent concentration. Again and again he drew back to begin the attack on the combination again; he worked with enduring patience as Z-7 and Tim Donovan watched. Long, anxious minutes passed before he straightened alertly, and spun the wheel geared to the giant bolts.

It whirled. The bolts withdrew from their sockets. Operator 5 pulled upon the weighty door. When it swung wide, he stood peering into the depths of the vault. Z-7 and Tim Donovan, standing at his side, gazed in consternation into the thick-walled space.

On the floor a man lay. Barton Hildreth. His collar was torn open. His face was swollen horribly; his open eyes were protruding; his tongue was visible between his puffy lips. His whole face shone purple in the glare of the light. He seemed to stare with savage fury out of the vault at the men who gazed upon him in death.

"He killed himself deliberately, Chief," Jimmy Christopher said quietly. "The ventilator would have enabled him to live this long without the slightest difficulty. He shut off the supply of air as the only means of escape. There lies a man who dreamed of wielding a power of steel over all the world—dead within walls forged by his own furnaces!"

"Hildreth!" Z-7 exclaimed. "His death removes a great danger from the world. Without you, we might never have suspected that his diabolical plan was in operation. Now, thank God, we can prove the facts before the world!"

"In the drawers of those files, Chief," Operator 5 said quietly, "there will be such a weight of proof that the world must accept it. Every person on the face of the globe must hear of it. Every living person must be made to realize that this war was the weapon of that man—that the Single State will never exist, that the Dictatorship of the World will never be attained. The power of Barton Hildreth has gone with his life...."

ELECTRIFYING NEWS flashed around the world with the passing of hours—news that filled hearts with hope:

> Warring Nations Agree to Armistice!
> Big Guns Stilled as Rulers Confer!
> World Watches Conference at Geneva!

Within the great hall of the League of Nations, the most momentous conference in the history of the world took place. There, with the eyes of the world turned upon them, the leaders of the nations that had been at war, met. While the armistice pact quieted a battle-torn land, the great men of enemies and allies alike gathered for the remaking of history.

Around the great table, the dignitaries sat—men of grave mien, of heavy responsibility, representing their diversified governments. Scores of unofficial representatives added their numbers to the delegations. Hundreds of reporters crowded the balcony, intent upon each word spoken. The Premier of Great Britain, presiding over the conclave of nations, rapped for quiet as delegate after delegate concluded their promises to cooperate for peace, to listen to the message of high importance which had been promised them.

"We are met because the necessity of cooperation presses

upon us to save ourselves from certain disaster. The reason for that necessity is about to be presented to you. The evidence about to be offered to the nations of the world is of the highest significance, and it is only proper that it shall be presented by the man responsible for its discovery. I cannot name him. I can only assure you that he is a secret agent of the United States government."

Silence fell in the great hall of the League of Nations. Behind the rostrum, a door opened quietly. Electric surprise tightened the air as a young man entered—a young man whose face was covered by a mask of black velvet. He advanced across the platform and gazed into the faces of the world dignitaries. Utter quiet waited for his words.

"Gentlemen! To each of you, when I finish addressing you, will be furnished copies of documents which I was fortunate to discover. These are unquestionable proof of the existence of a gigantic armament ring—a combine of manufacturers of weapons of war more powerful than any other force in the world. It is the power which plunged you into the war. It is the power which has driven you toward utter destruction. It still exists; it must be destroyed!

"It can be destroyed, gentlemen, by the will of the people of the world, by your governments acting upon the expression of that will. You have made war not because your peoples wished it, but because the power of steel forced you into it. Facing these facts, you must withdraw from the arena. Armies will not fight to line the pockets of armament makers. Mothers will not give their sons into the furnace of war to add gold to the treasuries of the makers of arms. Governments will not be controlled to the point of destruction by the seekers of private profit derived from human slaughter. The evidence placed before you, gentlemen, must bring peace or it will bring the utter destruction of the governments each of you represents.

"You will consider this evidence well while the world at large considers it. I can only place it before you and retire. Your work, gentlemen, has just begun—and mine is finished!"

OPERATOR 5 turned slowly and left the platform. He entered the room behind the rostrum, sensing the electrifying effects of his words in the Hall of Nations. Z-7 and Tim Donovan, John Christopher and Diane Elliot hurried to him. They had crossed the Atlantic with him on his mission of presenting his findings to the League. Now, increasingly anxious, they awaited the verdict.

In the great Hall, there was complete silence save for the rustling of papers as each dignitary studied the copies of the documents prepared by Operator 5. The minutes lengthened into hours before the gavel of the Premier rapped. The voice that rang through the door was that of the Minister of Foreign Affairs of France.

"Gentlemen! This amazing evidence is conclusive! There is not the slightest doubt that our nations have become the victims of a destructive power. There can be only one possible step for us. We must seize control of the armament ring and reduce it to its parts; we must dismember the monster and kill it! My heart bleeds at the thought of the thousands of young men who have already died on the battlefields of this second World War;

it sings with joy when I think that we have reached a time of peace. Let us—"

"Peace!" the cry rang in the Hall.

Mounting voices chorused until the gavel in the hand of the British Premier stilled them. His solemn voice carried clearly as Jimmy Christopher listened. He announced that a vote upon a continuation of the armistice, without terms, would be conducted at once if the delegates desired, and a shout of assent followed. Again there was a rustling of papers, a mingling of tense voices. It lasted through a long period, as voice after voice rose in answer to the roll-call. Through the closed door, Operator 5 listened intently as, again, the gavel rapped.

The British Premier spoke again:

"Gentlemen—we now have peace!"

Z-7's hand sought Operator 5's. His black eyes smouldered; his eyes glowed with inexpressible admiration. Quietly through the surging cheers that filled the great Hall of Nations, he spoke: "You have wielded a power for peace greater than the Masked Power wielded for war! You deserve a place in history beside the greatest of men. I'm proud to shake your hand, Operator 5—proud!"

His blue eyes shining, Operator 5 listened to the cheers echoing in the Hall of Nations. His one hand closed tightly about Tim Donovan's, his other holding Diane Elliot's, a warm smile curved his lips....

IN HIS sumptuous penthouse apartment, Carleton Victor sat at dinner. Across a table laid with impeccable linen, glittering with finest crystal and silver, he gazed at the lovely girl who was his guest, Diane Elliot. Her hand stole across the table to his as they waited for the estimable Crowe to appear.

"Jimmy," she said quietly, "you've done so much—and the world can never know who deserves credit for your achievements. They don't know your name—they don't know your face. It's so unfair, Jimmy—your having to work under cover of absolute secrecy—never to receive any reward for what you've done."

"Your eyes, Diane," said Carleton Victor, "give me the highest reward I could wish. What I see in them is more precious to me than any decoration or fame could possibly be. You, and Tim, and Dad—what more could anyone hope for?"

"Jimmy Christopher—!"

"I'm afraid," Carleton Victor said quietly, "Crowe might hear, Diane. Where is he? We've finished—he's never neglected me before like this." He called. "Crowe! Where the devil are you?"

The startled manservant burst into the room, wide-eyed, carrying a newspaper in his hands. Remembering it, he tossed it aside and hurried to the table.

"I beg your pardon, sir!" he blurted. "Most careless of me! I shall bring the coffee at once, sir! It's the first newspaper I've seen in ten years, Mr. Victor—I never look at them—but it was lying in the bedroom, and the headlines—"

"You found them interesting, Crowe?"

"Yes, sir! Very, sir! Most astonishing. The masked young man who appeared before the League of Nations and presented evidence that stopped the war—by Jove, sir, he must be a most remarkable young fellow. His identity a complete mystery, too!... Your coffee at once sir!... I wonder who he is?"

Diane Elliot's eyes twinkled. Carleton Victor raised his napkin to cover a smile. "I wonder, too, Crowe," he said quietly.

www.ingramcontent.com/pod-product-compliance
Lightning Source LLC
Chambersburg PA
CBHW020407180626
46812CB00003B/874